SPUR AWARD

"___
—Joe ___ of
Dead in the West

After a long, successful career in the fields of horror, fantasy, and science fiction legend . . . author Richard Matheson his remarkable talents to one of his favorite genres—the Western. His first Western novel was an incredible success, the winner of the Golden Spur Award for Best Western Novel of 1991 . . .

JOURNAL OF THE GUN YEARS

An epic adventure from the diary of Marshall Clay Halser, a gunfighter who lived up to his legend . . . and died for it.

"THE BEST NOVEL I READ LAST YEAR."
—**Stephen King**

"BREATHTAKING . . . FIRST RATE . . . IMPOSSIBLE TO PUT DOWN."   —**Spur Award–winner Richard Wheeler**

"A THREE-CARAT DIAMOND. READ AND ENJOY IT WITHOUT DELAY."   —**Max Evans, winner of the Levis Strauss Golden Saddleman Award**

"A REMARKABLE WESTERN NOVEL . . . HIGH EXCITEMENT."   —**Spur Award–winner Norman Zollinger**

"A SPECTACULAR CREATION."
—**Dale Walker, columnist,
Rocky Mountain News**

"THE AUTHOR GIVES HIS STORY A CREDIBILITY AND HONESTY UNUSUAL IN THE GENRE."
—***Publishers Weekly***

"SOME OF THE BEST DAMN WRITING MATHESON'S DONE IN A SPECTACULAR CAREER."
—**Loren Estleman, author of *Bloody Season***

Turn the page for more rave reviews . . .

THE GUNFIGHT

Richard Matheson's powerful novel of a young girl's idle gossip—and the explosive reaction of a small town—that leads to dishonor and death . . .

"TIMELESS HUMAN DRAMA . . . IMMEDIATE AND COMPELLING."
—Booklist

"PAGE-TURNING . . . THIS IS AN ABSORBING PARABLE about the terrible effects of gossip and the tragedy of a peaceable man driven to violence."
—Publishers Weekly

"ANOTHER WESTERN TRIUMPH FOR RICHARD MATHESON."
—Spur Award–winner Norman Zollinger

"RAW, ROUGH, AND REAL."
—Loren Estleman

"SUPERBLY WRITTEN SUSPENSE!"
—Library Journal

"SURPRISING AND MOVING . . . AN EMINENTLY SATISFYING PIECE OF WORK."
—Spur Award–winner Chad Oliver

"REAL PEOPLE, PLOT TWISTS, AND AUTHENTIC WESTERN COLOR . . . A VERY, VERY GOOD BOOK."
—Ed Gorman

"A DECEPTIVELY SIMPLE PREMISE . . . AN UNFORGETTABLE CHARACTER . . . MATHESON MAKES EVERYTHING WORK."
—Dale Walker, *Rocky Mountain News*

And now, Richard Matheson once again proves his storytelling genius with an exciting collection of classic Western tales, together for the first time in one volume . . .

BY THE GUN

Berkley Books by Richard Matheson

JOURNAL OF THE GUN YEARS
THE GUNFIGHT
BY THE GUN

BY THE GUN

RICHARD MATHESON

BERKLEY BOOKS, NEW YORK

"Gunsight" was previously published in *Dime Western* in 1951.
"Go West, Young Man" first appeared in *Bluebook* magazine in 1954.
"Boy in the Rocks" first appeared in *Western* magazine in December 1955.
"Too Proud to Lose" first appeared in *Fifteen Western Tales* in February 1955.

BY THE GUN

A Berkley Book / published by arrangement with
RXR, Inc.

PRINTING HISTORY
Berkley edition / February 1994

ISBN 0-425-14099-7

BERKLEY®
Berkley Books are published by The Berkley Publishing Group,
200 Madison Avenue, New York, New York 10016.
BERKLEY and the "B" design
are trademarks belonging to Berkley Publishing Corporation.

PRINTED IN THE UNITED STATES OF AMERICA

10 9 8 7 6 5 4 3 2 1

To the gang:
Nick and Judy Perito,
Walt and Dody Steiner,
Brian and Bunny Herdeg . . .
for many years of love and laughter.

CONTENTS

GUNSIGHT

1

One-Man Law

DOING MY ROUNDS makes me thirsty. So I usually stop in at the Bobolink Saloon in between Mrs. Girty's rheumatism and my afternoon office hours.

This particular day—the date don't occur to me—I had just give Mrs. Girty a talk and some harmless pills. So I found myself pushing through the flapping doors of the Bobolink, saying hello to the boys and stepping up to my private spot at the brown wood bar.

Wasn't much of an unusual day, no trouble, no excitement. Not that I wanted any, you understand. It's just a comment. No, the peace and quiet that Sheriff John Cooley kept in Bobolink was more than satisfactory to this coot.

About a week before we'd had a little fracas, nothing much. Didn't even happen in town, and John didn't hear of it till later.

One of the Douglas boys—Jim it was, the younger one—had lost his temper and challenged Tom Vesey of the Bar-X ranch to a little shooting duel.

It was a short one. To our surprise, Tom winged the kid in

the right shoulder and let it go at that; didn't even try and kill him.

So, at the moment Jim was out in his cabin where he and his brother Matt lived.

Outside of that, there wasn't nothing doing in town. And even *that* little upset had been the first in about seven years. Of course, there were always fistfights when the Douglas brothers came visiting. But there was no gunning while John Cooley was around.

I often wonder what kind of a town Bobolink would be today if young John hadn't decided to stay in town that day eighteen years ago and accept the office of sheriff. It's nice wondering. For my money, the town would be a ghost now instead of a right thriving little community.

At any rate, someone would sure have shot me long ago for being a horse doctor that changed his line.

Well, anyway, there I was, my foot on the rail while Mickey, the bartender, poured me my usual *libation*. Read that in a book once.

Tom Vesey had the misfortune to be in town that day picking up a few supplies for the ranch he worked on.

He was at the other end of the bar tossing off a few. It was dim and cool in the saloon, hardly no sound at all but the clicking of chips and a few remarks at the poker game. It was peaceful.

I was just making about my thousandth examination of the fat nude painting over the bar when I heard the swing doors pushed open and heavy boots on the floor. I paid no mind, being what you might call absorbed in higher study.

But then I heard one of the poker players mutter, "Uh-oh," and heard chairs scraped back and boots making for doors.

I turned around and took me a look.

There was Matt Douglas, all six foot three of him, a

mountain of a man with a face that looked like it was blasted out of a mountainside.

He was standing near the door and scowling at Tom Vesey. The way he looked, I felt mighty glad all of a sudden that my name is Doc Wheeler, I'm fifty-nine, and I don't carry guns.

Mickey looked pained and muttered to himself. He never could get over the memories of how often the Douglas boys had started fist battles there and cracked the mirrors, shattered bottles and glasses, and broken furniture. It wasn't exactly parsimony, I don't think. He just felt that fixings ought to get a honest chance to let time break them down.

Tom was staring back now. I'm sure he was scared. It was one thing facing down a hotheaded kid. It was another to face down the kid's brother who had an all-fired uncomfortable reputation.

"Hear you're the one laid up my brother," said Matt Douglas in his chilly baritone.

Tom's throat sort of moved like he was trying to swallow his last drink and not much succeeding. He licked his lips and looked white and grim.

"Now wait a second, Matt," he tried. "I could have killed Jim if I wanted. I only winged him on purpose. You gotta admit I could have killed him."

Matt didn't say nothing. He came up to the bar, and his fish eyes flicked over to me.

"Get out, Doc," he said.

"Now look, son—" I started to say. It must have been habit. I sure had no intention to try and stop the man in his business.

"Get out," he said again and, knowing better, I got. As I pushed through the door, I heard Matt Douglas saying:

5

"So you think I'm gonna thank you for putting a slug in his shoulder, huh? You think that, huh?"

I waited for the shots.

Outside the door, I stopped and looked back in.

They was facing each other, each one tensed for the other to draw. I felt strong that Matt wouldn't move first, that he knew full well he had the advantage. So he waited, calm and mean. I couldn't see his face, but I'll vow it had a twisted smile on it. He was that sort of coyote.

The moments passed, and it was something awful to stand there and hear the pendulum clock ticking one of their lives away. When a gunslinging happens fast, like it most often does, it's over before you get any time for the creeps. *Bang bang!* and there's two dead men or one or a couple of wounded ones and business for me. The shock is just a little one. Seeing a dead man isn't so bad when you're used to it.

But waiting and knowing there's about to be a dead man is something else again.

It's a funny feeling. The feeling that there's life in a man, his blood is pulsing through his veins, his heart is beating fast, and he's as alive as he'll ever be, all keyed up and scared.

Then you know at the same time that, in seconds maybe, that man will be as dead as he can be, his heart will stop sudden and his blood will run all over the floor.

And that waiting is the terrible thing. Waiting is always the worst.

I kept looking in, holding my breath. Matt didn't make a move. He was gaining advantage every second. He knew he wouldn't blow up. But it was obvious Tom would. I could almost see the sweat breaking out on his face, almost feel it. His hands trembled bad; you can't pull a gun smooth when your hand is shaking.

Then—*bang!*

Tom's hand fell, closed over the butt of his gun. Matt's hand swooped down; there was two blurs of light, two crashing shots echoing in the bar, two thinning puffs of smoke.

And Matt Douglas was still standing there, tall and hard as a rock.

But Tom Vesey's gun had slipped out of his fingers and banged on the floor. His eyes got a faraway, helpless look. His head lolled back and his knees sagged. He crumpled into a heap, and I saw blood pumping out of the big hole in his chest. That was it.

I went in then. Matt whirled and, to this day, I don't know what kept him from plugging me.

"What do you want?" he snarled.

"I'm a doc," I said. "Remember? The man looks like he needs one."

"He don't need nothin' but a box!" Matt snapped. "Get outta here!"

I stepped out again and watched. Far off I could hear shouting and faint bootsteps on the wooden sidewalk. Someone shouted, "Sheriff's coming!" I felt better.

While I waited for John to arrive, I watched Matt Douglas. Mickey had popped up again from behind his counter and was looking, too.

Matt walked slowly toward Tom's body.

I saw him stick a big boot under Tom's body and toss him over. Tom was flipped on his back, his arms banging on the floor.

I ain't much for feelings. But I got sick.

There's low and there's low.

You can't go no lower than spitting in a dead man's face.

"Sheriff's coming!"

7

The shout was repeated again, voices echoed it from the stores and stables and the hotel.

I turned my head and saw John Cooley approaching down the street, walking steady and calm. Easy to see why people shouted when he came. He was a man to give men confidence. For eighteen years he'd seen to it that Bobolink was the most lawful town in the state.

I watched him coming. His long mustache seemed to bristle with stubborn anger. His shoulder, his chin, his stance, even the crown of his hat—they were all square. That was the feeling he always gave me; an unbeatable square of man. He wasn't a big man. But every inch of him was packed with fire.

He stepped up on the walk and nodded at me.

"It's Matt Douglas," I told him, and he nodded again as he went in. His eyes didn't make any sign. They were always like that, distant and never showing for a second what was going on inside John Cooley.

I followed him in and stood in a corner.

John walked to the bar and stood there, his feet planted firm on the floor.

Matt Douglas looked over, then finished his drink slow. He didn't scare easy. But I don't think he felt too good then.

"You aim to shoot it out with me or you comin' peaceful?" John said, as if he was talking to a boy he found stealing apples.

Matt Douglas put down his glass and turned. "I had rights to shoot Tom Vesey," he said. "He bushwhacked my kid brother."

"He wasn't bushwhacked, and no one has rights to shoot anyone in Bobolink while I'm sheriff."

So there it was settled. I moved back in the shadows to wait. I knew it had to come. Douglas wouldn't ever give up.

This time it wasn't long. Because John didn't have no ideas about scaring other men into nervousness. He was sheriff, and he'd been defied. That was all there was to it. He made his move, a step forward.

It was then I got my first hint of something wrong. For John stumbled right into the bar rail and almost tripped himself. For the most surefooted man I ever seen, that was uncommon poor judgment of time to get clumsy. It almost did him in.

Matt Douglas wasn't no man to waste a moment like that. He jerked out his gun quick and let go. If it wasn't that John was off balance and lurching to the side to get his footing, that bullet would have tore a hole through his chest. As it was, he was knocked around by the bullet as it banged into his left shoulder.

Almost in the same moment, he got his gun out and fired.

Matt Douglas reeled against the bar with his hand clapped over his side, the blood streaming through his fingers.

And again I wondered. Because it was the first time I'd seen John Cooley miss a center shot. You could have almost called it a lucky hit if you dared, knowing what a dead eye John always had.

Well, anyway, Matt was out of the fight. John straightened up and backed to the door.

"McGee!" he bellowed.

McGee, the young deputy, ran in.

"Take Douglas and stick him in the pokey," said John. Then he grimaced and pushed his hand against the wound in his shoulder.

"You want to fix this, Doc?" he asked. And the way he said it, I really had a choice, as though he could manage somehow if I had more important matters. Hardest man to faze that I ever knew.

"Let's go," I said.

McGee led Douglas across the dusty street toward the jail, and John and I followed. Douglas kept peering over his shoulder at John, kind of curious. John kept his head down.

Clouds of powdery dust rose around us like ghosts. Someone on the hotel porch whooped and hollered when he saw Douglas staggering and beaten. Matt snapped his head around to see who it was. Then it was silent as a grave. No one wanted Matt Douglas mad at him, John Cooley or no.

At the jail McGee put Matt in a cell so I could patch him up without risk. Then McGee went to get the coroner. John stood watching, gun drawn while I took out the slug in Matt and bandaged him.

Matt didn't say nothing, not even when my knife was digging into him. But I could feel how tense and crazy he was. Sometimes I wonder what kept him from blowing up right then and there and trying to get loose, even wounded and held down with a gun. Then, other times, I figure a cruel life had been a hard teacher to him and that he knew when to fight and when to wait.

After Matt was bandaged, John and I left the cell and went in the next room. John sat down in his chair, I pulled up another.

"Lend me your knife, John," I said. "Mine's bloody."

He pulled the knife out of his belt sheath, and I slit open his shirt.

Nor did John make a sound while I gouged for the bullet. His brown face went white and he bit blood out of his lower lip. But he didn't say a thing.

"What kind of man," I asked him while I probed, "would spit on the face of a man he just shot?"

He clenched his teeth at the pain. "Crazy man," he gasped after I pulled out the slug.

Then something else strange happened.

As I raised the knife, the sunlight through the window reflected on the blade and the glare shone right in John's eyes. He hardly blinked. It seemed he was carrying this stubborn business a little too far.

I shone the glare in his eyes again.

Then he blinked and turned his head. "What are you doing?" he asked.

I bent over and tried to look in his eyes. He turned his head away.

"Bandage me," he said. "I got work to do."

I bandaged him and told him to come to my office that night so I could check on the shoulder. He was disgusted at that, but I made him promise to come.

There was something I wanted to find out.

John brought Mrs. Cooley with him that night. He was still mad about all this concern over his shoulder. He wasn't used to it.

"Let's get it over with," he said irritably, starting to unbutton his shirt.

"Never mind the shirt," I said.

He looked surprised at me. He squinted.

"What's the joke?" he asked. Then he glanced quick at his wife. "Sarah," he said, "you didn't—"

"No, John, I swear I never did," she said.

"Then it's true," I said. I didn't know anything was true or untrue, but I always found that people talk about things they think you know already.

John was reaching for his hat, but Sarah put her hand on his arm. "Sam is our friend," she said. She was the only person in town ever called me by my name.

John hesitated. I could feel how it riled him to give up on anything, even a secret that wasn't a secret anymore.

Finally he turned. "All right, Doc," he said. "I'll tell you because I'm counting on you to do something for me."

So I examined his eyes.

"How long has this been going on?" I asked.

"Few years," he said. "Gets worse and worse."

"And you never told anyone."

"You think I'm going to spread it round that I can't see good? Can you see me wearing specs? I'd be plugged in a week."

I fingered my beard, just downright astonished.

"You mean to tell me," I said, "you went barging into that bar to gunfight Matt Douglas when you could hardly even *see* him?"

"I had to," he said. And to John Cooley, that was the answer.

"How you hit him at all," I said, "I don't—" Then I just stopped talking.

"Matt Douglas?" Sarah cut in, horrified. "John, you told me—"

That was one of the few times I ever saw John Cooley look flustered. "Now Sarah," he said, "you'd have just worried if you knew."

"Oh, this is too much," she said, angry. "Too consarn much. You stubborn jackass! You'd do any fool thing rather than say you couldn't. If you aren't—"

She stumbled over the rest and couldn't finish.

"Well, now we know, John," I said. "Ain't it time you retired?"

"Retired!"

That got him. He stood up and glared at me.

"You know if I retired, this town would be shot wide

open," he growled. "Every drifter and gunman in this territory is just waiting for me to leave. All I have to do is retire and the Douglas brothers would be mayor and sheriff in a week!"

I wished I could argue with him. But I couldn't. It was all too true. Out of all the men in town, there wasn't one to match John. Even in his forties, with his graying hair, with his bowlegs—even with bad eyes—there still wasn't no other man in town I cared to see wearing his badge. Not a one.

"But John," I said anyway, "I know you're right, even Sarah can't say different. But you're walking yourself into the graveyard. Someone's bound to find out sooner or later. And that'll be your last day as sheriff."

He pushed a lean finger under his mustache. "Well," he said, "seems like I'm going to get shot whether I tell or not. So I think I'll just *not* tell and let everybody guess it. It'll take a spell longer."

"John, for heaven's sake," Sarah begged. "Will you try and get some sense in that rock head of yours—just for once?"

John didn't say nothing. Sarah wrung her hands together.

"Look, John," I said, "why not just leave town, go on a vacation? No one will know then."

Sarah looked anxiously at him. But I guess we knew what he'd say before he answered. He had that stubborn look on his face. "I ain't leaving town on my feet," he said. We knew what he meant.

We stood there awhile without talking. Then John said he had things to do. "I'll drop by tomorrow," he said, "to talk over how you can cure me."

Sarah and I stood listening while his boots clacked away on the sidewalk as he headed for the jail. There wasn't any hesitation in his step. He seemed as spry as ever, knew exactly where he was going.

I took Sarah home. And while we walked, she told me of the little signs she'd noticed at home, how long it had taken John to admit, even to himself, that something was happening to his sight.

While she was talking, I happened to think of Matt Douglas.

It made me shudder to think of him knowing that John Cooley was going blind.

John was at my office at exactly the time he said. He sat down, and I poured us a drink. He downed his and looked at me. "Well, Doc," he said, "what can you do for me?"

I looked at him a long moment, without speaking.

He was quick to understand. The ends of his mouth drooped for a moment. But then the old stubborn look was back on his face.

"You sure?" he said. "You plumb certain?"

I nodded. He pushed his lips together tight. I told him, without fancy words, without false hopes.

He never said a word. Then he sank back in the chair and looked at the floor. We sat there a few minutes without a sound.

Then I spoke. "Well, John," I said, "what are you going to do?"

He raised his eyes. "I'm staying," he said.

I didn't say anything. I wasn't surprised.

He went on talking, filling his shaken mind with the comfort of little details. He talked about how he'd saved money for Sarah, what he planned to do about a replacement if he got it.

"And most important," he finished, "I want to get Matt

14

Douglas sent over to the penitentiary. Then, too, I got to wait till Jim comes gunning for me and try to calm him down."

"That all?" I said.

He pulled his chair closer to mine. I couldn't help feeling that his eyes were as keen as before.

"Doc," he said, "can you tell me how long I'll be able to see at all?"

"I wouldn't want to say definite, John," I said. "It could be a year, maybe months, less even. Depends on how you treat them eyes."

He clenched his fists. "I ain't pampering them," he said.

I asked him how he expected to fool anyone, keep them from learning. He'd bump into doors, into people; he'd get more and more helpless. And sooner or later, someone who wanted him dead would find out.

"Listen, Doc," he said. "I have it worked out. Things are slow lately."

"Sure," I said, "only two shootings yesterday."

"They were the first in a long time," he said. "Fact is, the town is pretty settled. Has been for a long time. I can afford to keep my rounds down to just about nothing, leave all the legwork to McGee, just come around when something special happens."

He paused. "You know," he said, "in eighteen years of walking through the same little town, the same streets, the same stairs, halls, rooms, I got to know every spot. I can go anywhere with my eyes closed. I've done it. Last night I walked around the whole town with my eyes shut, and I didn't bump into a thing."

"What about people and horses?" I said. "They don't stand still."

"That's where I need your help."

15

"What can I do?" I said. "If folks see me walking with you all the time, they'll begin to wonder."

"I don't mean for you to be with me all the time," he said. "I want you to help me hear better."

"How's that?"

"A blind man has to hear good," he said. "As of now, I got good ears. But not good enough to judge distance and direction by sound. I want you to help me do that."

"You want to do that just to stay sheriff and get shot?"

He stood up. "I ain't getting shot," he said. "And you know I'm the only one can keep the town lawful. You helping me?"

I hesitated. Then I clapped him on the shoulder, the good one. No use struggling. "All right, Sheriff," I said. "I think we're both crazy, but I'll help you."

2
Boot Hill's Greetings

Ain't much point in going into long details of how John and me worked it out.

But it was *work*, no doubt of it. Long weeks of work that got lost in months. Work with always the thought hanging over us that pretty soon Jim Douglas would be coming into town for revenge.

There was a valley up in the hills where the Indians used to have a meeting place long about twenty years before. There was an old trapper's cabin there. We used that cabin a lot, went there most every day. John shot it full of holes.

I kept telling John he couldn't possibly get to hear a man drawing his gun, it just didn't make that much noise. I kept telling him the first thing he'd hear would be the roar of another gun and then a slug would tear his insides out.

"That when you're planning to make your move?" I'd ask him.

"Never mind," he'd say. "You just do like I say."

No use trying to argue down John Cooley. That's just one of the things a man can't do—like eat rocks and fly.

• • •

I used a long fishing pole and, from the hook, I dangled a five-pound weight which John had made up at the smith's. We'd be in the cabin, keeping all the light out by covering the windows.

I'd stand to one side and hold out the pole and swing the weight against a wall. John would fire at the shot. At first we didn't keep score, just let him get used to firing at sound.

But then we put up a white canvas on the wall and dipped the weight in black paint. I'd swing it, the weight would hit the canvas-covered wall, and John would fire. Then we'd pull aside the window cover and see how close he got. When we started he never even came near it.

But John willed he'd get better. And he did. After weeks of aching effort, he finally started hitting close to those black smears.

By that time, the price of bullets in Bobolink was rising fast and my shoulders and back muscles were about to snap. I couldn't sleep of nights for the ache in them, even though John rubbed me down with liniment.

I remember the day John blew the middle right out of the smear I put on the canvas.

We'd let in the light and was standing before the canvas. He leaned forward and squinted. "Did I hit it?" he asked. "I can't see good in this poor light."

I felt mighty strange. He was right next to the canvas, but he couldn't see the hole. And yet he was the sheriff of our town and every gunman in the section wanted him dead.

"You hit it, John," I said. "What now?"

At first I thought John was fooling.

I'd already lost weight standing in that black cabin listening to bullets whistle around me like the Furies.

John wasn't satisfied.

We were sitting on a sun-spotted rock. We'd just left the cabin where John had punctured nineteen spots out of twenty-five tries.

"Well, I guess that does it," I said.

"Nosir," he said. I lifted my eyes as John handed me a chaw. I took a bite, and we sat munching a spell.

"All right," I said. "What's on your mind?"

"I gotta learn to shoot at the sound of a man's voice," he told me.

"Why, sure," I said. "I'll just stand over there and say something and you take a shot at me. If you don't hit me the first time, why then we'll just practice over and over till you kill me."

John never cracked a smile, never saw him smile once. He spit out a little juice. "You ain't gonna get killed," he said.

He got up and I followed him toward a line of boulders. He stumbled a few times while he walked. I made sure not to notice. Of course he never said anything. Even once when he tripped and fell on his knees. He just jumped up and kept walking like nothing happened. But I could feel him fighting it every inch of the way, holding it in tight.

"What now?" I asked when we reached the boulders.

"You stand behind me," he said. "You yell, then duck. I'll wait a second after you yell, then I'll shoot."

"Sounds fine," I said, "if I don't forget to duck."

"You won't forget," he said, walking away. I thought I heard him add, "I hope." If that was his sense of humor, I'm kind of glad he kept it hid.

So we started on the new game. I'd yell and duck. He'd fire. He got pretty good at it, then mighty good. After a while I could talk real low and, the second after, a slug would zing off the top of the rock and sail into the sky.

Then John learned to shoot on the draw at my voice and got good at that.

Of course, while all this was going on, weeks was passing. Matt Douglas was getting madder and madder, Jim's shoulder was getting better along with John's. And all this stalling wasn't stopping any of these things from piling up and getting ready to explode.

It was like John said as we rode in one night from a long hard day of trying to shoot me. "Seems like a lot of doing for nothing, don't it?" he said.

I was too tired to be surprised, even though it was way out of line for John Cooley to doubt himself.

"John," I said, "just don't tell me after all this time that what we done was a waste."

He looked ahead grimly. "It weren't no waste," he said. "I'll be using it. Soon."

That made my stomach draw in, made a chill run over me, sweat-covered as I was.

Because John wasn't no young man and he was almost blind.

But he was planning to face a young killer with eyes like a hawk's.

It sort of didn't balance.

And then Jim Douglas *was* ready for his play. And it happened. John and I were in the jail when McGee came running through the doorway and gasped out that Jim had ridden into town and was in the saloon waiting for things to crack.

John sat quiet for about half a minute, fingering the hilt of his knife. Then he raised his eyes. "Stay here, McGee," he said. "Come on, Doc."

We left the jail and started up the street. "So you're still meaning to go through with it."

"Did you think I wouldn't?"

"No," I said.

We kept walking. I said, "I thought you said you was gonna try and calm him down."

John stopped across the street from the saloon. "I can't," he said. "If I could see good, I could wing him. But the way I learned, I'm bound to hit right under his voice and that'll probably kill him."

He leaned against the front of the general store. "You go over," he said. "Try and talk him into backing down and going back to his cabin. If he won't, tell him I'll meet him in the square."

I started to say something. But John, as always, was more than my match. I turned and started across the street.

"And don't beg," he said loudly. I kept walking, thinking how that was John's philosophy of life right there.

I stepped up on the walk and pushed through the doors of the Bobolink.

It was empty, almost. Mickey stood in back of the bar with that hurt look on his face again, the one that he gets when his fixtures are in peril. Standing at the bar was Jim Douglas, shorter and leaner than his brother.

I wasn't halfway through the door before his guns were out. All in all, that was a mighty risky minute I went through.

"What do you want?" he asked me, sliding his guns back.

I went up next to him and ordered a round for two.

"John Cooley sent me," I told him.

"What's the matter?" he sneered. "Afraid to come himself?"

Jim was a good-looking kid. But cruelty had twisted his

features and lined his face with meanness until it didn't rub off.

I smiled kind of mysterious as a bluff, figuring that John could use every advantage he could get. "Ever know him to be afraid of anything?" I said.

"Then where is he?"

I tried to talk him out of it, scare him out of it. He was like his brother. He wouldn't buy.

Finally I patted the bar with a weary hand. "All right, son," I said. "He's waiting in the square. I hope you're ready to meet your Maker."

He made a scornful sound and left quick. I followed him out and hurried down to the barbershop where I could watch the square. I said hello to the men standing inside. They were all at the three windows looking out in silence. I noticed as I stepped up to a window that Matt Douglas could see what was going on from his cell.

"What do you think, Doc?" asked one of the men.

"Nothing to worry about," I said.

Jim Douglas was walking across the dusty street. Standing in front of the jail was John. I don't suppose nobody but me noticed how strained his face was, as though he was trying to hear something a mile away.

He heard Jim's spurs clinking.

"Jim Douglas," he said, holding his hands in the air by his sides.

Jim stopped. His back was to me so I couldn't see his face. But he had good eyes. He must have wondered why John kept looking at the ground. John had to. If he looked in the wrong direction, Jim would know right away he couldn't see him.

"Draw your guns, Sheriff," Jim said, not without a little doubt in his voice.

"Use your head, Douglas," John said. "You got no reason to fight me."

"Let my brother out then."

"Your brother killed a man," John said. He had Jim located now, his eyes were raised.

"Then draw your guns," Jim said. I could see he was scared of not doing what he came into town for.

From the jail Matt Douglas suddenly yelled out, "Stop talking! Kill him!"

Jim's head snapped over. "Matt!" he said.

"Kill him!" Matt screeched.

That did it. Jim lifted his hands.

"Dra—" He started to say "draw," but that was as far as he got. John's gun was out and blazing before Jim's hands had reached the butts of his guns. He was caught square in the chest with two shots. He twisted around in agony and looked once toward his brother. Then he fell backwards.

"Cooley!" Matt screamed. "I'll get you for that!" His hands got white clutching the bars.

John walked slowly toward Jim's body. I hurried out of the shop and reached it first.

"Right here, John," I said.

"Thought I saw a blur," he said. "Is he dead?"

I bent over. Jim Douglas was staring up at John. There was a cold sweat on his face. I didn't know whether he was alive or not at first. Then I felt a feeble beating in his chest.

"Just about dead," I said.

"McGee!" John yelled.

McGee came running out of the jail. John stood by and followed while McGee and I carried Jim into the jail.

"Cooley!" Matt yelled from his cell. "Let me see him!

23

God help you if he's still alive and you won't let me see him!"

John sank down on the edge of his desk with a heavy sigh.

"Anything can be done?" he asked.

I told him Jim would be dead in minutes.

"Let Matt see him," John said.

McGee put Jim in the cell next to Matt's, laying him back on the bunk. Matt stared at his brother with his mouth open.

"Jimmy," he said in a broken voice. Jim groaned. Matt fell on his knees and clutched at his brother's hand. His face twitched in fear, the only time I ever saw that, saw that he was a man like all of us.

"Fix him up!" he shouted at me.

"It's too late," I told him.

"No!" he roared. "Fix him up or I'll kill you!"

"He's going to die," I said. "You should have thought of him before you went after Tom Vesey."

"You dirty son of a—" he began to say. Then his eyes flashed past me to the next room.

"Cooley!" he yelled. "I'll spit on your dead face yet!"

Jim said something, and Matt turned to him, suddenly changed back to a scared brother. I saw Jim's eyes flutter open. He tried to say something, but his gray lips hardly moved. He finally got it out, I guess, because Matt threw a sudden glance at me, his face blank with surprise.

I should have figured it out, but I didn't; I was never a smart one.

I turned and left Matt with his dying brother. Fifteen minutes later, Jim was dead.

3

Blind Man's Last Try

A MONTH PASSED. Matt's side was healed, and John had sent for a marshal to take him to the state penitentiary. The town was quiet and orderly.

John's eyesight had got worse and worse. I tried everything I could to help. But it weren't no use because the thing was too much started before John took the trouble to tell me about it.

I remember the morning John didn't show up at the jail. I went out to his house. Sarah let me in, her face puffy with crying. She pointed to the bedroom, and I went in.

John was sitting on the edge of their bed with only a pair of jeans on. He seemed to be staring out the window at the tree in his backyard. The muscles of his lean torso stood out in tense ridges.

But there wasn't no fight in him. Though he straightened up when he heard my footsteps, I had seen the droop of his shoulders. It was a shock. I never thought of John getting old till that moment.

"It's me, John," I said.

He rubbed a hand over his mouth, brushed down his mustache.

"Well," he said, "it's happened."

I stood him at the window and let the sun fall on his eyes. He didn't blink, didn't see. He was blind.

I sat down on the bed next to him then. Words seemed useless. "Well," I said, after a while, "you still meaning to stay?"

He took a deep breath. "No," he said. "Ain't no use kidding myself. I'll have to leave. Soon as the marshal takes Douglas."

I sat there without a word in my head. Finally I did all I could think of, patted him on the shoulder.

"You deserve a rest," I said, and left the room.

Sarah was standing by the front room window, looking out. "It's all over, isn't it?" she asked.

"Yes."

"He wouldn't tell me," she said, "but I knew it. Even John can't hide all the hurt in him."

I patted her shoulder, too. That was all the good I turned out in those moments. Just pat shoulders and shut up.

"He's going to quit," I said. "The two of you can go away."

"Thank heaven for that, anyway," she said. "He's alive. And maybe it's broken a little of that awful stubbornness in him."

She sobbed. "Oh, God," she muttered, "I hope it hasn't. I hope it hasn't."

It happened two days before the marshal was supposed to show up and take Matt.

I was in the barbershop taking a shave, leaning back in the chair, feeling tired and comfortable.

Suddenly a shot rang out, then two more. I lurched forward in the chair, almost getting my throat cut. I jumped up and ran to the window with the barber. We looked toward the jail, and I felt a cold sinking in my stomach. I tore the towel off my neck.

Then I ran out of the shop in my shirtsleeves and across the street. Several people were staring toward the jail.

I never thought for a second what I might be getting myself in for. I just ran. All I could think of was John, blind and, for all his clever tricks, still helpless against surprise.

I burst through the door, noticed the side door was wide open.

There was someone sprawled in the back room by the cell. I ran back.

It was McGee. From three holes in his chest blood pumped across his shirt and on the floor. I tossed a look around. He was gone! And I knew where he was going.

I was about to run out and warn John when I noticed McGee's face.

Matt Douglas wasn't in such a hurry that he couldn't show himself for what he was.

There, hanging from McGee's white cheek was a little glob of bubbly spit.

I ran out quick and started as fast as I could for John's house. People kept on trying to stop me and ask questions. I pushed past them and kept running, down the middle of the street, raising clouds of dust.

I was out of breath and covered with rolling sweat as I ran into John's front yard and dashed up on the porch.

The front door was wide open. I guess I must have felt pretty brave that day. I ran right in.

Sarah was in the living room, just struggling up from the

floor. As I ran to her and helped her up, I saw a dark blue welt under her right eye, another bruise on her cheek.

She dug her strong fingers into my arm. "Sam!" she cried. "Matt Douglas knows!"

"About John?"

"Yes, yes!" she said, her lips shaking. "He was here, looking for John. He . . . he said . . ."

"What, what?"

She pulled herself together. "He s-said he was going to . . . to *kill the blind man*. Oh, Sam, we have to stop John. He won't back down. You know he won't."

I helped her over to the couch.

"I tried to stop Matt," she said. "He hit me. Never mind me. Go and find John! Please find him."

I ran out without saying good-bye. I started legging it back down Main Street. I asked people if they'd seen John. No one had. When I ran past the jail, I saw men crowded around McGee's body. I kept on running.

I ran up and down the streets looking, calling, hoping that I wouldn't run into Matt.

Once I did have to duck in a doorway and press myself into a shadow as he came running past, gun in hand, another in his belt, his face red with a wild rage.

I was about ready to collapse when I saw John riding into town. I yelled to him and puffed over. He got off his horse and I ran up to him.

"John," I gasped, "Matt Douglas is loose. He's looking for you." I sucked in breath. "And he knows about your eyes," I said.

His mouth tightened. "Where is he?" he asked.

I stared at him, not believing my ears.

"Did you hear me?" I asked. "He knows you're blind!"

28

"Will you hold my horse, Doc," he said, "while I go find him?"

"For God's sake!" I yelled. "What's the matter with you? Haven't you got any—"

"I'm the sheriff!"

The defiant words shut me up. It was the first time I ever saw him really mad, his lean face taut with anger.

"I'm the sheriff," he repeated. "And while I am, no killer is running loose in Bobolink."

"But, John," I said, "what can you do?"

John handed me the reins and started walking away. He said something as he walked toward certain death.

"I can die without crying," he said.

"Sheriff's coming!"

The shout billowed ahead of him and echoed through town. The streets started to empty fast. Wagons rolled into side alleys, mothers scooted their youngsters inside buildings, storekeepers who were quick enough put boards over their front windows. The rest just pulled down their shades and hoped for straight shooting.

I found Sarah on the walk. Before I could say a word, she saw John walking down the middle of the street, his hands hanging tensely at his sides. The butts of his gun and knife glittered in the sun.

Sarah ran to him and grabbed his arm. "I'm not letting you do it," she said, her voice filled with angry fear. "You can't."

He kept walking. She couldn't hold him back.

"John," she cried, "for God's sake, stop!"

His fists clenched and his lips trembled with fury. He said something I couldn't hear, and she let go and stood alone and small in the street watching her husband walk toward the empty, silent square. I ran out and got her. We went back on the walk and hurried to the edge of the square.

John was in the middle of it, listening carefully. There wasn't a sound. He looked puzzled. He turned around, cupped his hand behind his ear. There wasn't a sound anywhere.

Then, suddenly, before John realized what was happening, Matt Douglas came charging out on horseback. As we watched, in stunned terror, a rope flicked over John's body and the noose tightened. John's arms were pinned and he was jerked off his feet and dragged around the dusty square in a great circle.

Sarah screamed and lurched forward. I held her back. I felt sick. Matt Douglas was going to make the most of John's blindness before he killed him. I looked around and saw almost all the people in town watching from windows and shadowed alleys. There was sick confusion in their faces. John Cooley was their sheriff, their safety. He'd never been topped before. And now Matt Douglas, a maniacal killer, was dragging their sheriff around the square at rope's end.

John kept trying to get on his feet, but Douglas kept the horse moving too fast. Around and around he galloped, looking back and laughing his loud crazy laugh to see the sheriff dragging and plunging through the dust.

I saw John struggle to pull his knife out. He kept lurching on the ground, his arms banging. His face scraped over the ground, came up with an ugly dirty scrape across one cheek.

"Stop it!" shrieked Sarah, pressing her hands against her cheeks.

I grabbed her arms and felt how she shook.

But there was nothing to be done. There wasn't a man in

town who'd dare try and stop Douglas. I didn't even have a gun.

Then it suddenly ended. John's knife flashed in the air, the rope was sliced through, and John rolled to a stop. He lay quiet, his chest heaving with breaths. Matt Douglas skidded the horse to a halt and jumped down. John stood up dizzily and felt for his gun. He took it out.

I felt my scalp crawl.

Matt Douglas was sitting on the walk and calmly pulling his boots off. There was a crazy smile of triumph on his face. He kept looking at John and laughing to himself.

Then he got up and walked quietly out into the square. Everything was deadly quiet.

"You can't win," John called to him, trying to make him shout.

Matt clapped his paws over his mouth and laughed like a crazy kid, his broad shoulders shaking.

He was going to play a game. We were going to have to stand and watch him toy with John before he killed him.

I threw a look around. Wasn't there one man in town worth his salt who'd defend John? I knew the answer.

Douglas started his game.

"Cooley!" he cried, and John fired.

But Matt had jumped to the side with a laugh. John fired at the laugh. Matt jumped again. The second shot winged into the dust. People around the square started ducking into buildings.

"Cooley!" Douglas taunted.

John fired again, his teeth clenched. The shot crashed through a distant window. Douglas laughed loud, jumped. The shot dug into the roof over me.

John was helpless. When his six shots were gone, he had

to reload. While he did, Matt sat down on the wooden walk and waited.

"Douglas, for the love of mercy," Sarah begged, "haven't you any heart?"

"Stop it!" I told her. "Don't make it worse for John than it is."

She was quiet. She would say no more, I felt.

John was too proud. It was killing him to be made a helpless fool. His face was drawn and tight, the color all gone. He made a pitiful sight, a smallish man with his white dusty clothes, his hat gone, the graying hair hanging wild over his forehead, blood running across his cheek.

He had his gun loaded. He stood waiting. Douglas got up and called out, jumped. But John didn't fire. He just started walking in the direction of Matt's voice. There was almost a crazed look on his face now, too. He wouldn't give up.

"Cooley!" Douglas shouted and hardly moved from the spot. John didn't fire, just shifted direction and kept walking.

It was a crazy scene, like a kids' game of blindman's bluff. Douglas running around, struggling to get his crazy humor out of the situation, John flowing doggedly, the gun held tightly in his hand.

"Coo—" Matt started again, furiously. John fired quick. The bullet kicked up dust a few inches from Matt. Matt dragged one gun out of his belt, his face twisted with fear.

Sarah gasped. I cursed myself for a coward, for not having the guts to try and stop it.

Douglas turned and ran crazily across the square. John fired at the sound of his running, almost hit him. Douglas stopped and whirled around. There was about fifty feet between them now.

Douglas raised his gun slowly and fired.

John spun around as the bullet crashed into his right shoulder. His gun fell into the dust. He slipped to his knees and felt around for it. Douglas fired again, and the gun kicked across the ground, half the butt shattered off. John crawled around on his knees like a furious child, his hands slapping at the ground, looking for his gun. I felt tears of powerless rage run down my cheeks. Matt Douglas threw back his head and shouted with laughter.

John found the gun and picked it up in his left hand. He struggled to his feet and started toward Matt. Matt's laughter died out, his face hardened. He raised his gun again and fired. John's right leg buckled under him and he fell on his side in the dust. Even across the way, I heard him draw in a whining breath of utter, helpless fury.

He started to crawl toward Douglas now, his teeth crushed together, the broken gun held clenched in his grimy hand.

I ran in the store behind me. Several men stood at the windows watching. I jerked a gun out of one man's holster and ran out before he could say anything. I pulled back the hammer and sent up a prayer that I could hit Matt Douglas.

As I ran out, I saw John Cooley struggle to his feet and waver. He raised his gun.

Matt Douglas had taken all he could. He couldn't stand watching John, shot up and blind, still coming for him. He was afraid, afraid of a helpless, sightless man. That's how strong John Cooley was.

Before I could do anything, Matt raised his gun and pumped two bullets into John's chest. John fired once, but the shot went wild as his body lurched under the impact of two slugs.

He stood wavering there. I felt everybody hold their breath. It was like seeing Justice totter.

33

Then John fell over, his face pressed against the street, his body still.

I thought my eyes would pop. Matt Douglas was walking toward John's body. And, in my mind, I saw the spit on Vesey's and McGee's faces.

I knew I'd rather die than see it. I jumped down in the street and ran toward Douglas. As he whirled, I fired. You'd think I couldn't miss.

But I missed.

He raised his gun quick and sent a bullet into my shoulder. I twisted around and fell to my knees. I wished he'd killed me, rather than left me with the power to watch him, watch in horror while he walked toward John.

Someone rushed up to me. Sarah grabbed the gun off the ground and held it up.

"Stop!" she cried in a wavering voice. "Or I'll shoot."

I tried to tell her to shoot first. But I could hardly talk. Matt whirled, pulled another gun from his belt, and shattered Sarah's arm. She cried out in pain.

It was all over. Sarah stood watching Douglas as he walked over to John.

Douglas looked around at everybody with a sneer on his face. Then, he casually stuck his boot under John's body and tossed him over like a sack of potatoes.

Three fast shots rang out.

Matt Douglas's mouth fell open, the spittle ran over his chin. He looked dazed and stupid.

He twisted around and stumbled away, his eyes still wide with stunned surprise. He raised one hand and then fell.

Sarah ran over to John, who still held the smoking gun tightly in his hands.

She fell on her knees by him. I fought my way up and staggered over.

John turned his cloudy eyes on us. He tried to smile at Sarah. Then he felt for my arm. He squeezed it weakly. He was covered with blood, shattered, blind, half-dead. But he mumbled through his red-spittled lips with all his stubborn pride.

"I ain't dyin'," he said.

And who was I to argue with a man of John Cooley's mind?

GO WEST,
YOUNG MAN

THE STAGE TO Grantville had only the two of us as passengers that afternoon, rocking and swaying in its dusty, hot confines. The young man sat across from me, one palm braced against the hard, dry leather of the seat, the other holding in his lap a small, black bag.

Outside, beneath the fiery Texas sun, the air was driven by the thunder of twenty-four pounding hooves, the skeleton rattle of doubletree chains, the wild groan of cradle springs, the creaking complaint of twisting woods. Inside, the two of us, jolting forward and back, breathing in the dust of the alkali flats that led to Grantville.

Grantville. I'm used to that name now. But, like every other rankling Confederate supporter, I hated the name for many years and, like them, insisted on calling the town by its old name—Davisville. I was still calling it that in 1871 when all this happened. But the anger was fading. Where there is timeless sorrow, anger soon departs.

But about the young man: I say he was a young man but only a stretch of point would have put him in the ranks of manhood. I think he was somewhere near nineteen or twenty, although I never really knew. His coloring was fair under the film of dust, and what part of his hair I could see beneath the narrow-brimmed hat was the color of freshly dropped chestnuts. He was dressed in checkered flannel and wore a dark tie with a stickpin in its center. His build was almost delicate and, from the manner of his dress, I knew he had no liking for the outdoors. He was a city boy.

Since we had left Austin two hours before, I had been rather interested in the bag he carried so attentively on his lap. I noticed how the gaze of his light blue eyes kept dropping down to it and how, every time they did, the thin-lipped mouth would twitch. But whether it was twitching toward a smile or a frown, I also never knew.

The young man had another bag in addition to the small one on his knees. This, he had placed on the seat beside him. It too was black, a little larger but, apparently, made by the same concern. This bag the young man did not pay as much attention to, although he had, in Austin, insisted on taking it, too, into the coach with him. Since Jeb Knowles, who drove the rig, had no other passengers scheduled, he allowed the point.

So there we were, that young man and I, crossing the flats for Grantville, neither of us having offered to speak in the time we rode together. I had, for almost an hour and a half, been trying to read the Austin paper, but now I laid it down beside me on the dusty seat and looked once more at the young man's tightly set face. I glanced down at the small bag in his lap and saw how his slender fingers were clenched around the bone handle.

Curiosity then? You may call it that. Call it being snoopy even, but forgive us when we are old for our lack of aloofness. I could say that there was something in the young man's face that reminded me of Lew or Tylan but, probably, there wasn't.

Whatever my reason or lack of it, I picked up the newspaper and held it out to him.

"Care to read my paper?" I asked him above the din of sounds.

There was no smile on his young face as he shook his head once. If anything, his mouth grew tighter until it was a line of almost bitter resolve. It is not often you see such an expression in the face of so young a man. It is too hard at that age to hold on to either bitterness or resolution; too easy to smile and laugh and soon forget the worst of evils.

Maybe that was why the young man seemed so unusual to me but, there again, you can as easily put it to the dwindling faculties of old age. Faculties which could not prevent me from further assuming the role of pesty old man.

"I'm through with it, if you'd like," I said.

"No, thank you," he answered curtly, and it might have been the rocking of the coach that shook his head again.

"Interesting story here," I went on, unable to rein in a runaway tongue. "Some Mexican claims to have shot young Wesley Hardin."

The young man's eyes raised up a moment from his bag and looked at me intently. Then they lowered to the bag again.

"Course I don't believe a word of it," I said. "The man's not born yet who'll put young John Wesley away." I clucked once in that strange not quite certain admiration we Southerners had for that young, incredible man. "And him only eighteen." I shook my head, remembering. "The war has bred strange men."

The young man did not choose to talk, I saw. I leaned

41

back against the jolting seat and watched him as he studiously avoided my eyes.

Still I would not stop. What is this strange compulsion of old men to share themselves? Perhaps they fear to lose their last years in emptiness, seeking to fill the dwindling moments with anything but lonely silence.

"You must have gold in that bag," I said to him, "to guard it so zealously."

It was a smile he gave me now, though a mirthless one.

"No, not gold," the young man said and, as he finished saying so, I saw him swallow once nervously.

I smiled and, like the old man that I am and was, struck in deeper the wedge of conversation.

"Going to Davisville?" I asked.

He looked confused a moment. Then the lines about his serious face relaxed. "Oh, you mean Grantville," he said, and I knew suddenly from his voice that he was no Southern man.

I did not speak then. I turned my head away and looked out stiffly across the endless flat, watching through the choking haze of alkali dust the bleached scrub which dotted the barren stretches. For a while, I felt myself tightened with that rigidity we Southerners contracted in the presence of our conquerors. It was a meaningless withdrawal. I know it now; I think I knew it then. It was just that pride can be a stupid strength in a man, filling him with bitterness when he had better to be up and doing, moving forward toward adjustment and not retreating into malice.

But there is something stronger than pride and that is loneliness. It was what made me look back to the young man and, once more, see in him something of my own two boys who gave their lives at Shiloh. I could not, deep in myself, hate the young man for being from a different part of our nation. Even then, imbued as I was with the stiff pride of the Confederate, I was not good at hating.

"Planning to live in . . . in Grantville?" I asked.

The young man's eyes had evaded mine since Austin, and so I could not tell if the glitter I saw in them was permanent or something of the moment.

"Just for a while," he said.

"Going on," I said. The young man nodded once and, it seemed, his fingers grew yet tighter on the bag he held so firmly in his lap.

"You're from the . . . North," I said, wondering if I would be doing better to keep silent and knowing full well that I could not.

The young man seemed to hesitate, and I was conscious of deliberation on his part. It seemed as if he were deciding whether he should speak freely to me or say nothing at all. I saw his hand work restlessly on the handle of the bag and, as the rig groaned its way across a level area, the other hand, too, gripped tightly at the handle.

"You want to see what I have in—" The young man blurted out the words suddenly and then stopped, his mouth tightening as if he were angry to have spoken.

"Well, I . . ." I didn't know what to say at his impulsive half-finished offer. At my age, one does not make the adjustment easily when a man changes his attitude so quickly.

The young man very obviously clutched at my indecision to say, "Well, never mind, you wouldn't be interested." And, though I suppose I could have said—yes, I want to see–somehow, I felt it would have done no good.

The young man leaned back and braced himself again as the coach bounced up a rock-strewn incline. Hot, blunt waves of dust-laden wind poured through the open windows at my side. The young man had rolled down the curtain on his side shortly after we'd left Austin.

"Got business in our town?" I asked, after blowing dust from my nose and wiping it from around my eyes and mouth.

He seemed to lean forward slightly then, although, again, it might have been the jostling of the coach.

"You live in Grantville?" he asked loudly as, overhead, Jeb shouted commands to his three teams and snapped the leather popper of his whip over their straining bodies.

I nodded. "Run a grocery there," I said, smiling at him. "Been visiting up north with my oldest son."

He didn't seem to hear what I had said. Across his face a look as intent as any I have ever seen moved suddenly.

"Can you tell me something?" he began. "Who's the quickest pistol man in your town?"

The question startled me because it seemed born of no idle curiosity. I could see that the young man was far more than ordinarily interested in my reply. He *was* leaning forward, his hands clutching, bloodless, at the handle of his small, black bag.

"Pistol man?" I asked him.

"Yes, who's the quickest in Grantville? Is it Hardin? Does he come there often? Or Longley? Do they come there?"

That was the moment I knew that something was not quite right in that young man. For, when he spoke those words, his face was strained and anxious beyond a natural eagerness. It was a strange expression for the face of a young man from the city.

"I'm afraid I don't know much about such things," I told him. "The town is rough enough; I'll be the first man to admit to that. But I go my own way and folks like me go theirs and we stay out of trouble."

"But what about Hardin?"

"I'm afraid I don't know about that either, young man," I said. "Although I do believe that someone said he was in Kansas now."

Disappointment. That was what I saw on that young man's face, although I couldn't tell why. But it was there—a keen and heartfelt disappointment.

"Oh," he said and sank back a little, the tautness of excitement gone from his mouth.

He looked up suddenly. "But there are pistol men there," he said, "*dangerous* men."

I looked at him for a moment, wishing, somehow, that I had kept to my paper and not let the garrulous displays of age get the better of me.

"There are such men," I said stiffly, "wherever you look in our ravaged South."

That was when I knew that my former feeling of half-admiration for Wesley Hardin was an uncertain feeling, because it was not real but a perverted admiration for his defiance of the occupational forces. Then, too, it was the admiration anyone might feel for the man who lives in peril, carelessly. It is an admiration which takes little note that such men usually die in peril—young and violently.

"Is there a sheriff in Grantville?" the young man asked me then.

"There is," I said, but, for some reason, did not add that Sheriff Cleat was hardly more than a figurehead, a man who feared his own shadow and kept his appointment only because the county fathers were too far away to come and see for themselves what a futile job their appointee was doing.

I didn't tell the young man that. Vaguely uneasy, I told him nothing more at all, and we were separated by silence again; me to my thoughts, he to his—whatever strange, twisted thoughts they were. He looked at his bag and fingered at the handle, and his narrow chest rose and fell with sudden lurches. I couldn't help but wonder why he was going to Grantville, why he asked me the odd questions he had.

And, more particularly, with a tightening of shapeless alarm, what he had in that black bag on his lap.

A creaking, a rattling, a blurred spinning of thick spokes. A shouting, a deafening clatter of hooves in the dust. Over the far rise, the buildings of Grantville were clustered and waiting.

A young man was coming to town.

Grantville in the postwar period was typical of those Texas towns that struggled in the limbo between lawlessness and settlement. Into its dusty streets rode men tense with the anger of defeat. The very air seemed charged with bitter resentments—resentments toward the occupying forces, toward the rabble-rousing carpetbaggers, toward the Negro blundering in his newfound liberty, and often, with that warped evaluation of the angry man, toward himself and toward his kind. Potential violence straddled Grantville like a vengeful colossus. Threatening death was everywhere. You could smell it when you walked. And the dust was often red with blood as men who were not quick enough served as sacrifice to gods of glorious despair.

In such a town I sold food to men who often died before their stomachs could digest it.

I did not see the young man for hours after Jeb braked up the stage before the Blue Buck Hotel. I saw him move across the ground and up the hotel porch steps, holding tightly to his two bags. Then some old friends greeted me and I forgot him. I chatted for a while and then I walked by the store and talked a while with Merton Winthrop, the young man I had entrusted the store to in my three weeks absence. I checked receipts, I checked the credit book, I checked the shipment ledger. The store was in good order, I was pleased to find. I told Merton he had done a commendable job and then I went home and cleaned up and put on fresh clothes.

I judge it was near four that afternoon when I pushed through the batwings of the Nellie Gold Saloon. By nature I am not, nor ever was, a heavy drinking man, but I had acquired for several years the pleasurable habit of sitting in the cool shadows of a corner table with a whiskey drink to tinker with. It was a way I'd found for lingering over minutes.

That particular afternoon I had chatted for a while with George P. Shaughnessy, the afternoon bartender, then retired to my usual table to dream a few pre-supper dreams and listen to the idle buzz of conversations and the click of chips in the back room poker game.

It was where I was when the young man entered.

In truth, when he first came in, I didn't recognize him. For what a strange, incredible altering in his dress and carriage. The city clothes were gone; instead of a flannel coat he wore a broadcloth shirt, pearl-buttoned; in place of flannel trousers there were dark, tight-fitting trousers whose calves plunged into glossy, high-heeled boots. On his head a broad-brimmed Stetson hat cast a shadow across his grimly set features.

His boot heels had clumped him almost to the bar before I recognized him, before I grew suddenly aware of what he had been keeping so guardedly in that small, black bag.

For, crossing on his narrow waist, riding low, a brace of

gun belts hung, sagging with the ten-odd pounds of two Colt .44's in their holsters.

I confess to staring at the transformation. Few men in Grantville wore two pistols, much less slender young city men just arrived in town. And, in my mind, I heard again the questions he had put to me, and I had to set my glass down for the sudden, unaccountable shaking of my hand.

The other customers of the Nellie Gold looked only briefly at the young man, then returned to their several attentions. George P. Shaughnessy looked up smiling, gave the customary unnecessary wipe across the immaculate mahogany of the bar top, and asked the young man's pleasure.

"Whiskey," the young man said.

"Any special kind now?" George asked.

"Any kind," the young man said, thumbing back his hat with studied carelessness.

It was when the amber fluid was almost to the glass top that the young man asked the question I had, somehow, known he would ask from the moment I had recognized him.

"Tell me, who's the quickest pistol man in town?"

George looked up. "I beg your pardon, mister?" was what he said.

The young man repeated the question, his face motionless.

"Now what does a fine young fellow like you want to know that for?" George asked him in a fatherly way.

It was like the tightening of hide across a drum top the way the skin grew taut across the young man's cheeks.

"I asked you a question," he said with unpleasant flatness. "Answer it."

The two closest customers cut off their talking to observe,

and I, for one, felt my hands grow cold upon the tabletop. There was something in the young man's voice, a ruthlessness heard so often in the voices of men who had deserted all gods or hope of gods.

But George's face still retained the bantering cast it almost always had except in extreme provocation.

"Are you going to answer my question?" the young man said, drawing back his hands and tensing them with light suggestiveness along the bar edge.

"What's your name, young man?" George asked.

I felt myself start as the young man's mouth grew hard and his eyes went cold beneath the shadowing brim of his hat.

Then the thinness of a calculating smile played a moment on his lips.

"My name is Riker," he said, as if, somehow, he expected this unknown name to strike terror into all our hearts.

"Well, young Mr. Riker, may I ask you why you want to know about the quickest pistol man in town?"

"Who *is* it?" There was no smile on Riker's lips now; it had faded quickly into that grim, unyielding line again. In back I noticed one of the three poker players peering across the top of the half-doors into the main saloon.

"Well now, there's Sheriff Cleat," George said, smiling. "I'd say he's about—"

His face went slack as suddenly there was a pistol pointing at his chest.

"Don't tell me lies," young Riker said in tightly restrained anger. "I know your sheriff is a yellow dog; a man at the hotel told me so. I want the *truth*."

He emphasized the word again with a sudden thumbing back of the hammer, and I saw George's face go white.

"Mr. Riker, you're making a very bad mistake," he said,

then twitched back as the long pistol barrel jabbed into his chest.

Riker's mouth was twisted with fury. "Are you going to *tell* me?" he raged. His young voice cracked in the middle of the sentence like the uncertain voice of an adolescent, and the cracking seemed to make him angrier yet.

"Selkirk," George said quickly, and I felt a shudder running down my back.

The young man drew back his pistol, another smile trembling for a moment on his lips. He threw across a nervous glance at where I sat but did not recognize me. Then his cold, blue eyes were on George again.

"Selkirk," he repeated. "What's the first name?"

"Barth," George told him, his voice having neither anger nor fear.

"Barth Selkirk." The young man spoke the name as though to fix it in his mind. Then he leaned forward quickly, his nostrils flaring, the thin line of his mouth once more grown rigid.

"You tell him I want to kill him," he said. "Tell him I . . ." He swallowed hastily and jammed his lips together. "Tonight," he said then. "Right here. At eight o'clock." He shoved out the pistol barrel again. "You *tell* him," he commanded.

George said nothing, and Riker backed away from the bar, glancing over his shoulder once to see where the doors were. As he retreated, the high heel of his right boot gave a little inward and he almost fell. As he staggered for balance, his pistol barrel pointed restlessly around the room and, in the rising color of his face, his eyes looked with nervous apprehension into every dark corner.

Then he was at the doors again, his chest rising and falling with heavy, forced breaths. Before our blinking eyes, the pistol seemed to leap back into its holster. Young Riker smiled uncertainly, obviously desperate to convey the impression that he was in full command of the moment.

"Tell him I don't like him," he said as if he were tossing out a casual reason for his intention to kill Selkirk. "Tell him he's a dirty rebel," he said in a breathless sounding voice. "Tell him . . . *tell him* I'm a Yankee and I *hate* all rebels!"

For another moment he stood before us in wavering defiance. Then, suddenly, he was gone and we were staring at the place where he had stood.

George broke the spell. We heard the clink of glass on glass as he poured himself a drink. We watched him swallow it in a single gulp. "Young fool," he said in somewhat confused ire.

I got up and went over to him.

"How do you like *that*?" he asked me, gesturing one big hand in the general direction of the doors. "How do you like that for a young fool?"

"What are you going to do?" I asked him, conscious of the two nearby men now sauntering with affected carelessness for the doors.

"What am I *supposed* to do?" George asked me. "Tell Selkirk, I guess."

I told George about my talk with young Riker and of his strange transformation from city boy to, apparently, self-appointed pistol killer.

"Well," George said when I was finished talking, "where does that leave me? I can't have a young fool like that angry with me. Do you know his triggers were filed to a hair? Did you see the way he slung that Colt of his?" He shook his head. "He's a fool," he said, "but a dangerous fool—one that a man can't let himself take chances with."

"Don't tell Selkirk," I asked him, "I'll go to the sheriff and—"

George interrupted with a sound of deep disgust and

waved an open palm at me. "Don't joke now, John," he told me. "You know that Cleat will do nothing. You know he hides his head under the pillow when there's a shooting in the air."

"But this would be a slaughter, George," I said. "Selkirk is a hardened killer, you know that for a fact."

George eyed me curiously. "Why are you concerned about it?" he asked me.

"Because he's a boy," I said. "Because he doesn't know what he's doing."

George shrugged. "The boy came in and asked for it himself, didn't he?" he said. "Besides, even if I say nothing, Selkirk will hear about it, you can be sure of that. Those two who just went out—don't you think *they'll* spread the word?"

A grim smile raised Shaughnessy's lips. "The boy will get his right," he said. "And the Lord have mercy on his soul."

We stood wordless in the murky silence. Outside we heard the hollow beat of loping horses, the chatter of men talking, the far-off clanging of the blacksmith's anvil. It was the life in our town—the headless current of it running on, oblivious to the coming of one more act of violence, one more destruction.

I walked home slowly with the taste of dust and restless dread in my mouth.

George was right. Word of the young stranger's challenge flew about the town as if the wind had blown it. And with the word, the threadbare symbol of our justice, Sheriff Cleat, sought the sanctuary of his house, having either scoffed at all storm warnings or ignored them in his practiced way.

But the storm *was* coming; everyone knew it. The people

who filled the square with their presence knew it, and the men thronging in the Nellie Gold who had managed to develop a thirst quite out of keeping with their normal desires—these men knew it. One thing was for certain—the business of a saloon always thrived when a killing was expected within its walls. Death seems a fascinating lure to men who can stand aside and watch it operate on someone else.

For my own case, I stationed myself near the entrance of the Nellie Gold, hoping that I might speak to young Riker, who had been in his hotel room all afternoon, alone.

At seven-thirty, Selkirk and his ruffian friends galloped to the hitching rack, tied up their snorting mounts, and went into the saloon. I heard the greetings offered them and their returning laughs and shouts. They were elated, all of them; that was not hard to see. Things had been dull for them in the past few months. Cleat offered no resistance, only smiling fatuously to their bullying insults. And, in the absence of any other man willing to draw his pistol on Barth Selkirk, the days had dragged for him and for his gang, who thrived on violence. Gambling and drinking and the company of Grantville's fallen women was not enough for these men. It was why they were all bubbling with excited anticipation that night.

While I stood waiting on the wooden sidewalk, endlessly drawing out my pocket watch, I heard the men shouting back and forth among themselves inside the saloon. Only the deep, measured voice of Barth Selkirk I did not hear. He did not shout or laugh then or ever. It was why he hovered like a menacing wraith across our town. For he spoke his frightening logic with the thunder of his pistols and all men knew it.

Time passed. It was the first time in my life that

impending death had taken on much immediacy to me. My boys had died a thousand miles from me, falling while, oblivious, I sold flour to the blacksmith's wife. My wife died slowly, passing in the peace of slumber, without a cry or a sob.

Yet now I was deeply in this fearful moment. Because I had spoken to young Riker, because—yes, I knew it now—he had reminded me of Lew, I now stood shivering in the darkness, my hands clammy in my coat pockets, in my stomach a hardening knot of dread. It is not death that frightens but the wait for its inexorable coming.

And then my watch read eight and, looking up, I heard his boots clumping on the wood in even, unhurried strides.

I stepped out from the shadows and moved toward him, and it seemed as if the people in the square had grown suddenly quiet. I sensed men's eyes on me as I walked toward Riker's approaching form. It was the distortion of nerves and darkness I knew but, somehow, he seemed taller than before as he walked along with measured steps, his small hands swinging tensely at his sides.

I stopped before him and, for a moment, he looked irritably confused. Then that smile that showed no humor flickered on his tightly drawn face.

"It's the grocery man," he said, his voice a dry and brittle sound.

I swallowed the cold tightness in my throat. "Son, you're making a mistake," I said. "A very bad mistake."

"Get out of my way," he told me curtly, his eyes glancing over my shoulder at the saloon.

"Son, *believe* me. Barth Selkirk is too much for you to—"

In the dull glowing of saloon light, the eyes he turned on me were the blue of frozen, lifeless things. My voice broke off and, without another word, I stepped aside to let him pass. When a man sees in another man's eyes the insensible determination that I saw in Riker's, it is best to step aside for there are no words that will affect such men.

A moment more he looked at me and then, with a drawing back of shoulder muscles, he started walking again and did not stop until he stood before the batwings of the Nellie Gold.

I moved closer, staring at the light and shadows of his face illuminated by the inside lamps. And it seemed as though, for the fraction of a moment, the mask of relentless cruelty fell from his features revealing, underneath, stark terror.

But it was only a moment, and I could not be certain I had really seen it. For, abruptly, the eyes caught fire again, the thin mouth tightened, and Riker shoved through the doors with one long stride.

Silence; utter ringing silence in that room. Even the scuffing of my boot heels sounded loud as I edged cautiously to the doors.

Then, as I reached them, there was that sudden rustling, thumping, jingling combination of sounds that indicated general withdrawal from the two opposing men.

I looked in carefully.

Riker stood erect, his back to me, looking toward the bar which now stood deserted save for one man.

Barth Selkirk was a tall man who looked even taller because of the black he wore. His hair was long and blond; it hung in thick ringlets beneath his wide-brimmed Stetson. He wore his pistol low on his right hip, the butt reversed, the holster thonged tightly to his thigh. His face was long and copper-tanned, his eyes as sky blue as Riker's, his mouth a motionless line beneath the well-trimmed length of his mustache.

55

I had never seen Abilene's Hickok, but the word had always been that Selkirk might have been his twin.

The two men eyed each other, and a heavy airlessness filled the room as though every watching man had ceased to function; their breaths frozen, their bodies petrified, only their eyes alive—shifting back and forth from man to man. It might have been a room of statues, so silently did each man stand.

Then I saw Selkirk's broad chest slowly expanding as it filled with air. And, as it slowly sank, his deep voice broke the silence with the impact of a hammer blow on glass.

"*Well?*" he said and let his boot slide off the brass rail and thump down onto the floor.

An instant pause. Then, suddenly, a gasping in that room as if one man had gasped instead of all.

For Selkirk's fingers, barely to the butt of his pistol, had turned to stone as he gaped dumbly at the brace of Colt's in Riker's hands.

"Why you dirty—" he started to say, but then his voice was lost in the deafening roar of pistol fire. His body flung back against the bar edge as if a club had struck him in the chest. He held there for a moment, his face blank with dumb astonishment. Then the second pistol kicked thundering in Riker's hand and Selkirk went flailing back helplessly, landing in a twisted heap.

Dazed, I looked at Selkirk's still body, staring at the great gush of blood from his torn chest. Then, my eyes were on Riker again as he stood veiled in acrid smoke before the staring man.

I heard him swallow. "My name is Riker," he said, his voice trembling in spite of efforts to control it. "Remember that. *Riker.*"

He backed off nervously, his left pistol holstered in a blur of movement, his right still pointed toward the crowd of men.

Then he was out of the saloon again, his face contorted with a mixture of fear and exultation as he turned and saw me standing there.

"Did you see it?" he asked me in a shaking voice. "Did you *see* it?"

I looked at him without a word as his head jerked to the side and he looked into the saloon again, his hands plummeting down like shot birds to his pistol butts.

Apparently he saw no menace, for instantly his eyes were back on me again, excited, pupils dilated.

"They won't forget me now, will they?" he said. "They'll remember my name. They'll be afraid of it."

He started to walk past me, then twitched to the side and leaned, with a sudden weakness, against the saloon wall, his chest heaving with breath, his blue eyes jumping around feverishly. Men turned quickly from those eyes, their throats moving nervously as they moved away.

Riker's throat seemed clogged; he kept gasping at the air as though he were choking.

He swallowed with difficulty. "Did you *see* it?" he asked me again, as if he were desperate to share his murderous triumph. "He didn't even get to pull his pistols—didn't even get to *pull* them." His lean chest shuddered with turbulent breath. "*That's* how," he gasped. "*That's* how to do it." Another gasp. "I showed them. I showed them all how to do it. I came from the city and I showed them how. I got the best one they had, *the best one*." His throat moved so quickly it made a dry, clicking sound. "I showed them," he muttered.

He looked around blinking. "Now I'll—"

He looked all around with frightened eyes as if an army

57

of silent killers were encircling him. His face went slack and he forced together his shaking lips.

"Get out of my way," he suddenly ordered and pushed me aside. I turned and watched him walk rapidly toward the hotel, looking to the sides and over his shoulder with quick jerks of his head, his hands half poised at his sides.

And I tried to understand young Riker, but I couldn't.

He was from the city, that I knew. Some city in the mass of cities had borne him. He had come to Grantville with the deliberate intention of singling out the fastest pistol man and killing him face-to-face. That made no sense to me. That seemed a purposeless desire.

And now what would he do? He had told me he was only going to be in Grantville for a while. I knew now that Selkirk was dead, that while was over.

Where would young Riker go next? And would the same scenes repeat themselves in the next town and the next and the next after that? The young city man arriving, changing outfits, asking for the most dangerous pistol man, meeting him—was that how it was going to be in every town? How long could such insanity last? How long before he met a man who would not lose the draw?

My mind was filled with these endless questions. But, over all, the single question—*why?* Why was he doing this? What calculating madness had driven him from the city to seek out death in this strange land?

While I stood there wondering, Barth Selkirk's men carried out the blood-soaked body and laid carefully across his horse the body of their slain god. I was so close to them that I could see his blond hair ruffling slowly in the night wind and hear his lifeblood spattering on the darkness of the street.

Then I saw the six men looking toward the Blue Buck

Hotel, their eyes glinting vengefully in the light from the Nellie Gold, and I heard their voices talking low. No words came clear to me as they murmured among themselves but, from the way they kept looking toward the hotel, I knew of what they spoke.

I drew back into the shadows again, thinking they might see me and carry their conversation elsewhere. I stood in the blackness watching, and it seemed I knew exactly what they intended even before one of their shadowy group slapped a palm against his pistol butt and said distinctly, *"Come on."*

I saw them move away slowly, the six of them, their voices suddenly stilled, their eyes directed at the hotel they were walking toward.

Foolishness again; it is an old man's failure. For suddenly, I found myself stepping from the shadows once again and turning the corner of the saloon, then running down the alley between the Nellie Gold and Pike's Saddlery, rushing through the squares of light cast by the saloon windows, then into darkness again. I had no idea why I was running. I seemed driven by an unseen force which clutched all reason from my mind, allowing only one thought sway— *warn him.*

I am very old now, but I was old then, too, and my breath was quickly lost. My mouth fell open and, running with frantic steps, I sucked in breaths of air to cool my aching throat and chest. I felt my coattails flapping like furious bird wings against my legs and each thudding bootfall drove a mail-gloved fist against my heart.

I don't know how I beat them there except that they were walking cautiously while I ran headlong along St. Vera Street and hurried in the back way of the hotel.

I rushed down the silent hallway, my bootheels thumping with irregular beat along the frayed rug.

Maxwell Tarrant was at the desk that night; I remember that clearly. He looked up with a start as I came running up to him.

"Why, Mr. Callaway," he said, "what are—"

"Which room is Riker in?" I gasped, feeling breath burn inside my throat like hot sparks jumping from a fire.

"Riker?" young Tarrant asked me.

"*Quickly*, boy!" I cried and cast a frightened glance toward the entranceway as the jar of bootheels sounded on the porch steps.

"Room twenty-seven," young Tarrant said, and I rushed for the stairs, begging him to stall the men who were coming in for Riker.

I was barely to the second floor when I heard the broken thudding of their bootsteps on the lobby floor. I rushed down the dimly lit hall and reaching the door to Room 27, I rapped urgently on its thin wood.

Inside, I heard a rustling sound, the sound of stockinged feet padding on the floor, then Riker's frail, trembling voice asking who it was.

"It's Callaway," I said, "the grocery man. Let me in, quickly, you're in danger."

"Get out of here," he ordered me, his young voice sounding thinner yet.

"God help you, boy, prepare yourself," I told him breathlessly. "Selkirk's men are coming for you."

I heard his sharp, involuntary gasp. "*No*," he said. "That isn't—" He drew in a rasping breath. "How *many*?" he asked me in a hollow tone.

"Six," I said, and on the other side of the door I thought I heard a sob.

"That isn't fair!" he burst out then in angry fright. "It's not fair, six against one. It isn't *fair*!"

I stood there for another moment, staring at the door, imagining that twisted young man on the other side, sick with terror, his heart jolting like club beats in his chest, able to think of nothing but a moral quality those six men never knew.

"What am I going to *do*?" He suddenly begged me for the answer.

I had no answer. For suddenly, I heard the thumping of their boots as they started up the stairs and, helpless in my age and in my impotence, I backed quickly from the door and scuttled, like the frightened thing I was, down the hall into the shadows there.

Like a dream it was, seeing those six grim-faced men come moving down the hall with a heavy trudging of boots, a thin jingling of spur rowels, in each of their hands a long Colt's pistol. No, like a nightmare, not a dream. Knowing that these living creatures were headed for the room in which young Riker waited. I felt something sinking in my stomach, something cold and wrenching at my insides. Helpless I was; I never knew such helplessness. For no seeming reason, I suddenly saw my Lew inside that room, waiting to be killed, and it made me tremble without the strength to stop.

Their boots halted. The six men ringed the door, three on one side, three on the other. Six young men, their faces tight with unyielding intention, their hands bloodless so firmly did they hold their pistols.

The silence broke. "Come out of that room, you Yankee bastard!" one of them said loudly. He was Thomas Ashwood, a boy I'd once seen playing children's games in the streets of Grantville, a boy who had grown into the twisted man who now stood, gun in hand, all thoughts driven from his mind but those of killing and revenge.

61

Silence for a moment.

"I said, *come out!*" Ashwood cried again, then jerked his body to the side as the hotel seemed to tremble with a deafening blast and one of the door panels exploded into jagged splinters.

As the slug gouged into papered plaster across the hall, Ashwood fired his pistol twice into the door lock, the double flash of light splashing up his cheeks like lightning. My ears rang with the explosions as they echoed and resounded, rolling up and down the hall.

Another pistol shot roared inside the room. Then, Ashwood kicked in the lock-splintered door and leapt out of my sight. The ear-shattering exchange of shots seemed to pin me to the wall.

Then, in the sudden silence, I heard young Riker cry out in a pitiful voice, "Don't shoot me any more!"

The next explosion hit me like a man's boot kicking at my stomach. I twitched back against the wall, my breath silenced as I watched the other men run into the room and heard the crashing thunder of their pistol fire.

It was over—all of it—in less than a minute. While I leaned weakly against the wall, hardly able to stand, I saw two of Selkirk's men help the wounded Ashwood down the hall, the other three walking behind, murmuring excitedly among themselves. One of them said, "We got him good."

In a moment, the sound of their boots was gone, and I stood alone in the empty hallway, staring blankly at the mist of powder smoke that drifted slowly from the open room.

I do not remember how long I stood there, my stomach a grinding twist of sickness, my hands trembling and cold at my sides.

Only when young Tarrant appeared, white-faced and

frightened at the head of the steps, did I find the strength to shuffle down the hall to Riker's room.

We found him lying in his blood, his pain-shocked eyes staring sightlessly at the ceiling, the two pistols still smoking in his rigid hands.

He was dressed in checkered flannel again, in white shirt and dark stockings, and it was grotesque to see him lying there that way, his city clothes covered with blood, those long pistols in his still, white hands.

"Oh God," young Tarrant said in a shocked whisper. "Why did they kill him?"

Although I knew, I shook my head and said nothing. I told young Tarrant to get the undertaker and said I would pay the costs. He was glad to leave that room.

I sat down on the bed, feeling very tired. I looked into young Riker's open bag and saw, inside, the shirts and underclothes, the ties and stockings.

It was in the bag I found the clippings and the diary.

The clippings were from Northern magazines and news-papers. They were about Hickok and Longley and Hardin and other famous pistol fighters of our territory. There were pencil marks drawn beneath certain sentences like *Wild Bill usually carries two derringers beneath his coat*, or *Many a man has lost his life because of Hardin's so-called "border roll" trick*. Sentences underlined in the way a student underlines those items in his text which he knows he must particularly remember.

The diary completed the picture. It told of a twisted mind holding up as idols those men whose only talent was to kill. It told of a young city boy who bought himself pistols and practiced drawing them from their holsters until he was incredibly quick, until his drawing speed became coupled with an ability to strike any target instantly.

It told of a projected odyssey in which a city boy would make himself the most famous pistol fighter in the South-west. It listed towns this same young man had meant to conquer.

Grantville was the first town on the list.

BOY IN THE ROCKS

1

THE HANDS OF the Circle Seven were just finishing up the great pot of black coffee when Frank Bollinger saw the far-off dust cloud.

"Looks like visitors," he said slowly, chewing up the last of his steak, then washing it down with coffee.

Most of the men glanced across the plain but were too weary to take much interest. Only their foreman, Rail Tiner, stood up, his eyes peering out across the darkening prairie.

"I told them damn fools to—" he started, then broke off and pressed his mouth into a tight, angry line. Abruptly, he glanced to the south where the beef herd was beginning to mill, and they all heard, faintly, the voices of the men on watch, trying to calm the restless cattle.

"Frank, ride out there and tell them damn fools I said not to bring them cows in till the mornin'," Tiner said.

Bollinger grunted twice, once in acknowledgment of the order, the second time indicating his exhaustion as he pushed to his feet, pulling his unbuckled gun belt up with him, and headed for the scattered remuda which was grazing a short distance from the camp.

Tiner stayed on his feet, looking tensely toward the scaling dust on the horizon while the rest of the men settled back on their elbows and backs, eyes shut, cigarette smoke curling in lazy wreaths above them, the light from the chuck wagon fire casting a flicker of shadows across their bronzed, motionless features. They paid no attention to their foreman or to the muffled curses which began drifting back to the camp as Frank Bollinger tried to saddle one of his horses.

Bollinger was just drawing in the hind cinch, his right foot shoved against the side of his mount, when hoofbeats sounded on the earth and, looking up, he saw an unfamiliar boy ride into the camp area. He finished bridling his apron-faced roan, then started walking it toward the fire.

The boy was sixteen at the most, seated on a panting buckskin pony, dressed in dust-covered flannel and wool, his hat looking as if it had suffered the pummeling crush of a stampede, the gun belt almost slipping over his hips.

As Bollinger entered the firelit area, he heard the boy answering Tiner.

"Hell, mister," the boy said, "how'd I know you was roundin' up out here? I ain't never been around here before. I'm just drivin' a few cows up north."

"You're alone?" Tiner asked, surprised.

"Sure enough," the boy answered, sounding almost belligerent. "Gonna fatten 'em up north and sell 'em."

"Well, you damn well better circle my herd wide, boy," Tiner warned. "I don't want your cows startin' no stampede."

"Don't worry none, mister, I'll circle your outfit," the boy said.

Tiner nodded. "Okay, boy," he said. "Care to light and put down some grub?"

"Like to," the boy said, "but I gotta get back to my cows."

"Wait a minute," said Tiner. The boy drew his pony around again. "Seein' as you're new to these parts," Tiner went on, "and just a one-man deal to the bargain, it'll only cost you ten dollars."

The boy's face went blank as he stared down at Tiner from the back of his shifting mount.

"What'd you say, mister?" he asked, but there wasn't a man there who thought he was asking a question. Some of them sat up or propped themselves on elbows, looking up interestedly at the lean, freckled face of the boy.

The corners of Rail Tiner's lips edged up a little, but he didn't say anything. Instead, with a casual gesture, he held out his left hand, palm up, toward the boy.

"This is free range." The boy's voice had become flat, stripped of emotion, and, although it was barely noticeable, the grip on his right-hand rein grew a little looser.

"Wrong," said Tiner, sounding amused. "This is Circle Seven range. Strangers pay. Or they don't cross." And he moved the outstretched fingers of his left hand a little as if beckoning in the money.

The boy's face was stone now, his body was like stone in the dark saddle.

"This is free range," he said.

Now all the men in the camp area were sitting up, watching attentively in the dim, smoke-pungent air.

"You ain't meanin' to pay then?" Tiner asked, sounding more amused than irritated.

"That's right," the boy said. "I ain't."

Tiner shrugged. His left hand moved down slowly to his side like the folded-in wing of a bird watching carrion.

"Okay, boy," he said. "Cash money ain't required. One o' your cows'll do for the crossin' price."

Sudden heated color sprang up the boy's cheeks. "Listen, mister, I drove these cows more'n four hundred miles. I chased off two thievin' bands o' Kiowas and one o' Comanches. I tussled with three wolves, five rattlers, and a cloudburst. You think I'm gonna give ya one o' my cows, you're loco!"

The smile was gone from Tiner's face as if it had been made of smoke. Eyes like black stones, he glanced over to the edge of the camp where Frank Bollinger stood beside his horse. His head jerked once in the general direction of the approaching herd.

"Go cut out a good one," Tiner said to Frank Bollinger. Then, without waiting to hear what the boy would say, he turned on his heel and walked toward the chuck wagon, spurs clinking on the hard ground.

"You ain't gonna *do* it," the boy said tensely as Bollinger swung up quickly into the saddle. "Mister, I'm warnin' ya. Leave my cows alone."

Bollinger laid reins across the roan's left side and nudged it with his knees into a slow canter away from the camp.

"Mister, I'm *warnin'* ya!" the boy shouted after him. Suddenly he dug his spurs in, making the buckskin pony charge out of the camp toward Bollinger's mount.

Several of the hands stood up to watch, and at the chuck wagon, Tiner turned his head quickly to see what the boy intended to do.

Frank Bollinger heard the sharp drumming of hooves behind him but kept moving forward, the pace of his roan quickening into a gallop. The boy raked spur wheels across his pony's flanks, and it leapt forward with a new burst of strength, head lowered, its legs drawn high, and pistoned at the earth in a blur of motion. Straight for Bollinger the pony swept. In the failing light, the Circle Seven hands saw the pony gain distance rapidly until, abruptly, it had cut across the path of Bollinger's roan and the two horses were rearing wildly, their sharp-edged hooves hammering at the air.

"Get back!" the boy yelled, his face twisted taut with fury.

Bollinger's answer was to let his right hand drop to his pistol butt. The boy's hand fell alike. Two eight-inch Colt barrels cleared their holsters almost simultaneously; two sharp explosions rocked the air. The boy's shot was first. Frank Bollinger was torn from his saddle and thrown to the earth like a rag doll stuffed with rocks.

A snorting bellow went up from the Circle Seven beef herd, and two scimitar-horned bulls lunged forward, great eyes dumb with fright.

"Mount up!" yelled Tiner, dropping his coffee cup and racing through the milling of hastily rising cowboys.

Out on the plain, the boy shoved his pistol back into his holster and, seeing the activity in camp, jerked his pony around and galloped off. The outer rank of Circle Seven longhorns started after him, the sound of their increasing run like that of thunder rising.

Now all the hands, exhaustion ignored, were thudding across the plain toward the remuda with the ungainly motion of high-heeled runners, heavy saddles slung across their shoulders. The men on herd watch had spurred forward and turned back the first tide of stampede, but now another bunch of cattle started off, one following another in thoughtless imitation.

"Hurry, damn it!" shouted Tiner.

The darkening sky was lashed by whipping lariats which fell across the heads of the scattering horses, adding their outraged whinnies to the lowing and earth-trembling hoof-beats of the stampeding herd. Saddles were thrown on and cinched, bridles adjusted with jerking motions; the hands mounted and rode off quickly to tighten up the herd.

It took all of them forty minutes to gather in and contain the frightened longhorns, and they were able to do that only because it was the first day of roundup and the beef herd was not too big.

Even more exhausted now, the men walked their ponies back toward the camp area. Tiner and two hands rode over to where the cook knelt beside Bollinger, who lay dying in the August heat, his blood-soaked chest laboring for breath.

A minute later, Tiner straightened up, and the three men looked at him without a word.

"Have 'im buried," Tiner said evenly to the cook, who nodded once. Then the copper-brown skin tightened across Tiner's cheekbones and he jerked his head toward the horses. "Let's go," was all he muttered, but the two hands understood perfectly. Hitching up their gun belts, they strode quickly for their mounts.

2

JODY FLANAGAN WAS honest. Hothead he was, truculent to a fault, one to take sudden and fiery offense; yet absolutely honest. Credit for that belonged to the mixed rearing he'd got from his parents, both dead now—his father, a wild-tempered Irish horsebreaker who died with a bullet in his back because no man dared attempt to put one in his front; his mother, a staff of fibrous strength around which she had formed an outward flesh of patient, Christian gentleness.

From this brew had been poured the integrity and volatile courage of Jody Flanagan.

Integrity made him thrust aside the constant temptation to build his herd from the unbranded strays of other men. While numerous of his contemporaries rode the spring-thawed range gathering in newborn calves—sometimes with their mothers; sometimes alone and bawling, their mothers lying shot and marble-eyed in the mud—Jody Flanagan had been socking away his forty dollars a month. He had avoided, also, that all too present temptation at pay time to ride hell-for-leather to the nearest town for the solace of liquor and women. Instead, he had lived the monastic life of the range and planned ahead.

Finally, the day had come when he had saved enough for his own herd—fifty head of stringy-muscled cows, and bulls with horns that thrust from their skulls like grappling hooks.

That was, almost to the day, Jody Flanagan's sixteenth birthday.

He had spent that spring and summer deep in the open range, nursing his herd along like a solicitous father, sleeping on the hard-baked sod at night, riding all day, shifting his herd around so they would have the best of grass, the best of water. With the help of two hired drifters, he had branded the cattle with his own brand, the *Lazy J-F*—a *J* lying wearily on its side with the arms of the *F* pointing earthward from its body.

Sleeping little, the waist of his pants getting slacker by the month, the color of his face deepening to a sun-scorched brown, his muscles becoming more and more like wire, Jody Flanagan had acquired reflexes like the nervous reactive jumping of a cat.

And then, after all that, some sidewinder had tried to take one of his hard-earned cows. It was the only man Jody Flanagan had ever killed, but he felt no regrets as he spurred back to his herd. As well as possible in the nearly obscuring darkness, he gathered in its drifting fringes.

That done, the longhorns bedded down for the night—some grazing, some snorting in a rhythmic sleep. Jody sat quietly on the pony, his black-barreled Henry repeater drawn from its quiver-shaped scabbard and lying across his saddle.

Grazing near him was his weary packhorse, still loaded in the event a sudden break became necessary. Far to his left,

Jody could hear the rapid, stone-whipping current of a narrow stream and the occasional snort of a drinking steer. On the other side of that stream, Jody had noticed before the fall of night, was a great pile of rocks which, by their massing, had formed a sort of barricaded cave.

The exhaustion of an all-day drive was deep in him. He was just starting to nod a little when the thud of approaching hooves caused his head to jerk up alertly. Two, three riders, he figured. The Henry rifle was drawn up tensely in his hands. He'd been expecting riders.

He held in the buckskin's nervous shifting with his knees and a gentle patting on its cool neck. "Easy girl," he whispered, his eyes straining to the impossible feat of penetrating the heavy blackness around him.

The hoofbeats were closer now; no more than a hundred yards away. Separated too, he judged. The riders must have split in order to thin out his potential target. Jody swallowed quickly and drew in a shaky breath. It wasn't fear, he knew, so much as not knowing exactly what he was up against.

Then Jody saw the shadowy bulk of the horse and its rider loom out of the night about fifteen yards from him.

With a rapid hand movement, he jerked the trigger-guard lever down and up, loading and cocking the rifle.

The horseman reined up instantly, a figure frozen to its saddle.

"Get out of—" was all Jody had time to say before the night exploded with pistol blasts and he heard the whistle of slugs passing his head.

The pony jerked out of control under him and his returned fire missed widely. His left hand clutched down at the horn-looped reins, his spur wheels dug into the flanks of the spooking buckskin. The other man had fired twice more before Jody jerked his mount around, aimed quickly at the barrel flashes, and squeezed the trigger. The Henry jolted in his grip, its explosion drowning out everything.

Then, in the sudden silence, he heard the strangled coughing of the hit rider and the telltale, rustling slide and thud of his body on the hard, night-shrouded earth.

There was no respite. Almost in that same moment, the other horsemen charged toward him, converging as they came. Heart thudding, Jody levered another shell into the Henry's chamber but held fire so as not to offer even a momentary flash of target. He heard the frightened bellow of his herd and worried for a second about them stampeding.

Then suddenly it occurred to him that the approaching riders might be decoys, that there might be Circle Seven men all around him, closing in slowly, unseen. Cautiously, he backed his pony toward the rushing sound of the stream, a dry swallow clicking in his throat. Thirsty, he thought, his canteen empty and no chance to fill it now.

His attackers moved closer, the muffled hoof thuds of their mounts indefinable in location. Jody clutched the rifle. His sharp eyes moved restlessly, trying to pick the riders out in the night.

He started as a sudden curse broke the silence, drowned in the very second of its utterance by a double blast of gunfire. In the fiery splashes of muzzle blast, Jody saw two men firing point-blank into something. Then, in the abruptly renewed darkness, Jody heard the agonized death screech of a horse as it stumbled heavily for a few yards, then went crashing to the earth.

"It's his damn *packhorse*!" someone growled.

Jody felt rage well up in him. Throwing the Henry to his shoulder, he rent the night with explosions, levering and firing in a paroxysm of fury until his trigger pull brought only the metallic click of the hammer.

Only then did he realize that some of the deafening gunfire was not his own, because the darkness was still alive with powder flashes, still torn by the roaring of gun blasts and the whistling of slugs around his head and body.

He shoved the Henry into its scabbard and was just drawing his Colt when scudding clouds unveiled the moon, and the broad prairie was bathed with a sudden chalky illumination.

In the hesitant moment before firing began again, Jody saw three dark figures; one man writhing on the ground, a second still seated on his horse, and on the fringes of his vision, the motionless bulk of his packhorse.

Then the night exploded again and a slug drove into Jody's left arm, almost knocking him from the saddle. In one synchronized movement, he clutched at the horn and spur-scraped his pony into a startled run. Upright then, he pulled up the reins and jerked the buckskin around as two more slugs burned past his head, one of them whipping through the brim of his hat.

Hastily, while his wounded arm was still numb, Jody shifted the reins and jerked out his Colt. He snapped off a shot at the lone rider and saw the hat go flying from his head like a dark bird suddenly rising.

He was about to reverse direction again in a sudden desire to end the battle when he heard the drumming of hoofbeats. Casting a glance to the side, he saw four more horsemen approaching at a dead gallop.

Bullets whizzing past him, he spurred his pony into a gallop toward the suddenly remembered pile of rocks. He fired once more over his shoulder. Then his pony was lurching and sliding down the gravel-strewn incline of the stream, its hooves striking white sparks from the stones.

Pain started in his left arm and Jody holstered his pistol,

shifting the reins again as the pony plunged into the moonlit current. More shots rang out, sending up crystal columns around him, sparking off stones.

The horse gained the other side of the stream where, with a bellow, one of Jody's steers lurched away into the shadow of the cottonwoods. Jody ignored it, throwing his right leg over the horn and dropping rapidly to the ground, taking the Henry with him.

Looking toward the opposite bank, he saw two of the five men ride into outline against the sky. Dropping the rifle, he jerked out his Colt and fired once. His mouth tightened in grim satisfaction as one of the men lurched in the saddle.

Jody tried to grab the saddlebags with his left hand and his teeth grated together, blocking the hiss of pain as red-hot pokers drove into the nerves around his wound.

Holstering his pistol, he dragged the saddlebags off the buckskin and swung them hard against its flank, sending it off with a startled whinny into the safety of the night.

Grabbing his rifle, Jody raced across the ground between him and the rock pile, bootheels crunching on the gravel, weaving his path a little to spoil the aim of the four men now on the opposite shore.

With a final lunge he dove into the shelter of the rocks, hearing the ping and whine of ricocheting bullets surrounding him.

There was abrupt silence then. Jody twisted around, again sliding the Colt from its holster; but the men were no longer silhouetted against the skyline.

He let his arm down and sat there on the damp ground, breathing raggedly, feeling waves of pain oscillate through his arm and into his shoulder. He licked his dry lips and glanced up at the moon. If only clouds would cover it, he might slip away—but the moon hung like a great white eye.

Fifteen yards away, Jody heard the tantalizing gurgle of fresh, running water. He closed his eyes and let his head sink forward until his forehead rested on the cool surface of the boulder. His arm hurt badly. He knew that the riders were going to take his herd and pin him down until he finally made a desperate run for it and was shot.

Yet none of these things seemed to matter so much as the sound of water in his ears.

A drink of water, he thought, just a little drink of water.

3

ON THE MORNING of August 22, 1895, crossing that portion of the Texas Panhandle which belonged, by the practical legality of power, to the Circle Seven ranch, three riders were driving a herd of seventy-five longhorns ahead of them.

Earlier that morning, the three men had combined their separate drives—twenty-five head apiece—and now were guiding the dust-raising herd toward the holding point of the Circle Seven's beef roundup.

The three were hands of the region's smaller ranches—Bob Service of the Flying O, Mack Thursday of the W Bench, and John Goodwill of the Walking Diamond. The longhorns moving calmly and evenly, the three men rode together into the hot, blunt, llano wind.

"I don't give a damn about that," young Bob Service was saying, "it's still robbery in my log."

Mack Thursday shrugged. He was the oldest of the three, forty-two, in the decline of his cowpunching career; a heavyset man with iron-gray hair and quiet eyes who sat his roan like a man who knew the seating of a horse better than the seating of a chair.

"Sure, it's robbery," Mack Thursday admitted, "but that don't change a thing."

"Open range," John Goodwill said in a disgusted voice, "what a pile o' chips that is." He was young, twenty-six, resentful.

"Open range," said Thursday, "only means it's open till some outfit with faster guns closes it." He raised his bandanna and wiped at the sweat on his forehead.

"And how long do we swallow it?" asked Bob Service, his face tight with anger. "How long do we bring cows to them to pay our way across a range that belongs to all of us?"

"Well—" Thursday started.

"What kind of range is it when three outfits take orders from one?" Service cut in. "What kind of range is it when you have to pay a bribe so you can drive your herds north? What kind of men are we to *take* it?"

"Yeah," agreed a vengeful John Goodwill. "Why the hell should we give away cows to them?"

"Take it easy," Thursday pacified. "Neither of you was here when the range war was on two years ago. Neither of you saw the good men that was killed for this godforsaken piece of earth. Well, I saw it."

He paused a moment, his mouth turning down at the ends.

"I saw my own boy torn to pieces by a scattergun," he said. "He looked so awful bad I couldn't even take him to his own mother. He's buried out here on the range he fought for—died for." His voice was husky and bitter. "Well, it didn't do no good. A lot of men died, but Circle Seven still owns the range. And, as for me, I'd rather see twenty-five cows paid up spring and fall than see good men blown to pieces for nothin'."

The men rode in silence a while, Service and Goodwill still looking angry, Thursday, tired and resigned.

"Well, I *wouldn't* rather see it," Service finally said. "No disrespect to you, Thursday; I know how you must feel losin' your boy and all but—hell, if things go on like this, what's to keep Tiner and his crew from askin' thirty head next spring, fifty in the fall, maybe a hundred the next spring?"

"Nothin' I guess," said Thursday. "Though I wouldn't go blamin' the Circle Seven men for this setup. It ain't their doin'. They're just cowhands like you and me. It's Tiner holds it together."

"What about old man Ralston?" Goodwill asked, referring to the owner of the powerful Circle Seven.

Thursday wiped at sweat again with his finger and shook it away. "As you said, Goodwill, he's an old man. He ain't got the powers of his mind no more. Tiner feeds him locoweed talk, puffs him up like a boy with his first hoss and pistol. That's all Ralston is, actually, a little boy who likes to feel strong. It's Tiner runs the show."

"Then why don't someone call him?" Service said, slapping once at the wood stock of his holstered Colt.

A grim smile edged up the lips of Thursday. "Always open season on him. Anyone's welcome to try and call Rail Tiner. Matter of fact, least a dozen men already have." The smile faded. "They're all buried," he said flatly, "and Tiner's still ridin'." He glanced at Service. "You figure on callin' him?" he asked. "I don't."

Bob Service was not the kind to spout loose talk. So, directly challenged, he shut up and rode in silence, thinking about what Thursday had said.

Thursday went on, "No, I believe my boss has the right idea. He herds a thousand, maybe fifteen hundred cows a year. He'd rather give up twenty-five of them than risk losin' everything."

"Ain't no gettin' ahead that way," grumbled Goodwill. "A man just holds hisself back thinkin' like that."

"Like I say," Thursday answered quietly, "you're welcome to try and end it."

"No lone-hand job'll end this setup," Service allowed himself to comment. "It'll take all of us."

"That's for sure," Thursday agreed somberly, "but all of us don't feel the same about it. Well," he said, shrugging wearily, "maybe somethin'll prod us to it. Let's hope for that."

"Hope ain't gonna end the setup either," Service growled as he nudged his pony into a trot toward the east fringe of the herd where several steers were drifting out toward a thick patch of grama grass.

Sensing that talk was ended, Goodwill moved away, too, and for the rest of the way, the three men remained apart, riding with their thoughts and sweating under the hot sun.

By eleven o'clock they were moving the herd along the low ridge which overlooked Double Fork River, only a narrow stream now after a virtually rainless summer. In the distance they could see the Circle Seven's beef herd and camp, minus the chuck wagon, which had been driven out onto the range to feed the hands.

They were almost to the holding spot when a single rider started out toward them. Service, riding lead, spurred forward to meet him. As the man drew closer, Service was surprised to see that it was Tiner. The foreman was usually on the range during the roundup.

Tiner reined up in front of him and, without any greeting, gestured toward the prairie with his left arm. "Get away from the riverbank," he ordered. "Edge 'em out and circle 'em into the rock corral."

"Why?" Service asked.

"You heard me!" Tiner snapped irritably, then turned away and galloped back toward his camp.

Thursday rode up to ask, "What's wrong?"

Service told him in a disgruntled voice. Thursday, after a mild shrug, rode back to the herd point with Service where they arranged themselves on both sides and, swerving slowly, guided the longhorns away from the riverbank.

"Who the hell's he think he *is*, bossin' us around?" Service asked above the sounds of the herd.

"Tiner," was Thursday's reply.

They were almost to the rock corral when a single rifle shot sounded near the river. The three men each threw a quick glance in that direction but were forced to concentrate on the startled cattle.

With the aid of one of the Circle Seven hands, they delivered the seventy-five longhorns to the natural rock corral where they would be culled for beef stock, the remainder set loose on the range, re-branded. When the herd was installed, John Goodwill rode over to Thursday and Service, looking excited.

"Ya know what that shot was?" he asked them.

"What?" Service asked.

"They got some young kid down there, no more'n sixteen, trapped in the rocks." He gestured toward the rock corral. "Them's his cows. Tiner took 'em."

For the first time that day, Thursday looked something more than taciturn. "*Took* 'em?"

Goodwill nodded. "That's what the fella told me."

"Why?" Thursday asked quickly, despite his practiced caution.

"Dunno," Goodwill answered, shaking his head. "I only talked to him half a minute. All I know is Tiner took the kid's cows after some shootin' and now the kid's holed up down in a bunch o' rocks."

A disturbed expression settled across Thursday's face. Even though he had struggled long to maintain a detached view of Circle Seven dominance, this new situation was too strong to ignore and reaction showed in the tenseness of his jaw, the fleeting pain in his eyes. Worried anger held him, anger he could not help experiencing even though he didn't want to.

But then it was submerged, pushed down by an anger of resolve equal to it, controlled before Service said in a low, thoughtful inciting voice:

"Maybe we're next."

Thursday glanced at him without a word, seeing on the young man's face the very tension he had repressed; and, sensing the ire which fanned across them, seeking to express itself in action, he cut it off—willfully, with jerked-in knees that stirred his mount away from them.

"Come on," he said bluntly, "let's get the receipts signed."

The circle of resentment snapped. Goodwill and Service rode after him, not speaking, in their eyes the look of men who were defeated not by battle but by the failure to enter battle.

As he rode toward the Circle Seven camp, Thursday's glance swept along the riverbank, settling, for a moment, on the man stretched out behind two rocks, a rifle poked into the opening between them. There was a bandage on the man's left arm that caught the sun's rays whitely. A boy in the rocks, he thought, and his eyes moved on hastily across the camp to the milling beef herd, to the mounted cowhand watching over them, his right arm in a bandanna sling.

The lines around Thursday's eyes deepened with worry, then grew still harsher as his glance settled on the two man-length mounds of freshly dug earth near the camp. Something restless plucked at his insides like a hand prodding him to something he had no desire to do. A word moved emptily inside him: coward. It made him sick and furious. He didn't believe it, but he couldn't avoid it.

Then, in the camp, he saw Tiner mount again and he veiled anger with attention to the tall man's approach.

"Paper, Thursday," Tiner said when he'd drawn up in front of the older man.

Thursday reached automatically for the pocket of his shirt as Goodwill and Service edged up beside him. Tiner jerked a stub of pencil from his vest pocket and scribbled initials on the receipt.

"Next," he said, and Goodwill handed across his slip of paper. "Pretty rotten lot of cows," Tiner added, initialing the second receipt.

Just in time, Thursday saw that Service was about to flare up and cut him off hastily.

"Who's the boy, Tiner?"

"Circle Seven business," Tiner answered, looking up irritably into the flinty eyes of Bob Service. "Come on, come on," he snapped, "I ain't got all day."

Flat insult hung in Service's voice. "If they're rotten cows," he said, "maybe you'd like us to take 'em back."

When the skin grew taut across Rail Tiner's face, it was as if someone were turning screws under the edges of it, tightening it quickly but evenly. It did something to his eyes; made them appear to start as if he were, for the first time, seeing the person that, till then, he had paid no attention to. "Your paper, cowboy," he said, lips hardly stirring, his left hand extended.

"Get it signed, man," Thursday said in abrupt urgency.

With a twisting of his mouth, Service jerked the receipt from his shirt pocket and held it out.

Tiner took it from him, his pale green eyes fixed to Service's face. "Thanks, cowboy," he said flatly. Without looking down once, he scrawled his initials largely across the receipt and handed it back, the smile he held from his lips showing in his eyes. It was a mocking smile.

"Who's the boy, Tiner?" Thursday asked again, anxious to get the foreman's attention off Service.

A moment longer, Tiner's static gaze clung to Service's face as if he were memorizing it. Then his eyes moved a little and settled on Thursday's broad, noncommittal face.

If either Service or Goodwill had asked the second time about something which Tiner had already announced as Circle Seven business, words would have ended in sudden movement, either fatal or near-fatal. But Thursday was one of the old ones. He and Tiner had known each other for ten years, they had fought each other in a bloody range war. Even opposed as they still were, there was something more between them than enmity. Grudge there was still, even hatred maybe, but, as enemies who had measured the values of each other in a time of violence, they respected more, allowed more.

"Some drifter," Tiner answered. "Wouldn't pay his way across the range. Killed a pair of my boys last night, shot up another pair. He even"—not without some grim amusement, he reached up an exploring finger—"put a hole in my new hat."

"Why'd you take his cows?" Thursday asked.

Tiner slid the short pencil into his vest pocket. "He ain't gonna need 'em where he's goin'," he said, one end of his mouth twitching slightly in what might have been the beginning of a smile.

"You're gonna *kill* him?" Thursday asked, wondering, almost nervously, what it was that made the blood pulse so heavily in his wrist and temple veins.

"Me or the heat," said Tiner, and from the tone of his voice, he might have been discussing dinner plans.

"Why? Because he wouldn't pay your damn price?" Service burst out, infuriated.

Studiedly, Tiner kept his eyes on Thursday's tense features. "Take your friends out of here," he said with that voice which grew less aroused the angrier he became. "Our deal is finished. Clear out."

"You think you can—" Service started, then was drowned out by Thursday's.

"That's enough! Let's go."

Both Goodwill and Service stared wordlessly at Thursday, despite their rising tempers, according him the respect due his unwritten rank as senior cowhand of the trio.

"See you in the spring," Tiner said casually, turning his horse and starting back for camp.

Thursday pulled his mount around. "Come on," he said, the anger in his voice more for himself than Service and Goodwill.

The three of them rode away at a slow trot, faces set in grim lines, eyes staring ahead bleakly into the endless oven blast of llano wind which buffeted their cheeks like scorching bird wings.

After a mile of tense silence, Thursday drew in a harsh breath. "All right, spit it out," he snapped. "Spit it out, damn it."

Service licked his upper lip slowly. "I was just thinkin' how hot it is. A man gets mighty thirsty in a sun like this."

Thursday pressed his lips together tightly, throat drawing in with a dry swallow. It wasn't the approach he'd expected or wanted. To be reminded of the boy, that he couldn't take. His Tom had been sixteen, too. A full-front scattergun blast had seen to it that Tom never saw seventeen.

Hastily, Thursday tried to lead Service to words he could combat. "And what did you think you were gonna do?" he asked in a clipped, angry voice. "Draw on Tiner?" He didn't wait for the answer. "You'd be dead now."

"Better dead than stepped on!" Service flared, giving Thursday the opening he wanted.

"*Think* a second, why don't you?" Thursday said sternly. "Is that the way you really feel? You'd rather be dead than alive? Dead with nothin' proved but your own bad judgment? Use your head, Service! You're no gunslinger. Ya didn't have a chance, not a damn chance, and you know it. I said it before, and I'll say it again: *There's no point to dyin' for nothin'!* I seen too many men go that way. I don't support it."

"And what *do* you support?" Service asked. "Knucklin' under? Lettin' yourself get shoved around like an animal? Lettin' a sixteen-year-old kid die when he ain't done a thing but fight for what was his?

"That kid might have a slug in him, Thursday, he might be bleedin' to death. Sure as hell he's dyin' of thirst. And here we go ridin' away like there was nothin' happenin'. Here we go ridin' away, talkin' like a pair of old ladies while that boy dies in them rocks!" Impulsively, Service jerked in his reins and glared at Thursday. "I'm goin' back. I'm gonna get that kid or a slug, either one. But I'm goin'."

"Man, use your—"

"No!" Service cut him off. "Talkin' don't mean nothin'. Words don't weigh enough to move the scales!"

"Man, if there's a thing to do," Thursday said quickly, not wanting to but unable to stop, "there's a right way and a wrong way. Gettin' killed for nothin' ain't the right way."

"It ain't for nothin'," Service said. "It's more than *nothin'* in them rocks." His head snapped to the side, his eyes lanced into Goodwill's. "What about it?" he asked.

Goodwill's mouth tightened. "I'm with it," he said huskily.

"Men, for God's sake!" Thursday burst out. "D'ya want to start another range war?"

"Come on," Service said through clenched teeth, pulling his mount around.

Thursday was silent. He sat motionless on his fidgeting horse, watching the two men gallop off. That core of tension in his stomach was expanding now. He felt as if he were turning to stone. He kept on saying it in his mind: They're wrong—they're wrong.

If only he could believe it.

4

RAIL TINER WAS checking over the seventy-five cattle when an air-bursting flurry of shots exploded from the river.

Jerking his head around, his startled gaze jumped down to where Jake Kettlebar was firing rapidly at something across the drought-thinned river.

With a muffled curse, Tiner jabbed in spurs, and his horse began shouldering its way through the shifting herd. Tiner looked angrily toward his beef herd. The cows hadn't had an hour's peace since that damned kid had shown up.

Reaching the end of the corral, Tiner jumped to the ground and took down the bar. Pulling his horse through the opening, he propped up the bar again. He mounted rapidly, started for the riverbank where the exchange of shots still raged. I thought he'd be dead by now, Tiner thought irritably. He'd have gone down to get the kid long before, except that the kid was too good with a gun. Two men buried, two wounded; that was enough loss to take for fifty scrawny cows and a worthless life.

When Tiner reached the bank, Jake Kettlebar was

slumped behind one of the boulders, reloading, grimacing tensely because of his leg. Rifle with him, Tiner slid to the ground, ignoring the dust-spattering slugs around him, and ran, crouched, to where Kettlebar was.

"What the hell now?" he yelled above the gun explosions.

"Two of them fellas that was just here," Kettlebar gasped, "they're tryin' to get that kid out of the rocks."

Rage flashed through Tiner. Face contorted, he jumped out and looked across the river to where the two men, pistols in hands, were rushing clumsily from rock to rock, trying to reach the boulder-piled cave where the boy was hiding. He noticed there was no movement or sound from the cave.

Then he yelled, "Get the hell out o' there!"

One of the two men dropped to his right knee and snapped off a shot that tore a strip of shirt from Tiner's left arm.

With a sudden, icy silence, Tiner threw the Winchester to his shoulder and fired once. Across the way, the man cried out involuntarily as the pistol flew from his hand.

Tiner saw the man clutch painfully at his wrist. Then, from the corner of his eye, Tiner saw the other man rear up behind a boulder. Shifting the rifle barrel with a blurred motion, Tiner fired again. The other man's shot went wild as Tiner's slug gouged away part of his right shoulder.

"Drop it!" Tiner yelled, but the man couldn't hold it anyway and the Colt dropped to the ground beside him. Tiner saw that he was the one who'd angered him over the receipt. For a moment, Tiner felt a sharp inclination to put a bullet in the man's chest.

Then, with a precautionary glance toward the rocks, Tiner let the Winchester's barrel droop, holding the rifle with one hand only. "Get over here," he ordered, "and don't get brave or I'll blow you both to pieces."

The two cowhands glanced at each other, then up at Tiner. They looked like guilty, sullen boys caught napping.

"Damn fools," Tiner muttered to himself as he watched them lurch across the gravel bed of the stream and clump, dripping, up the bank toward him, their eyes glancing back curiously toward the mass of rocks.

"Go get their pistols," Tiner told Kettlebar," "and see if the kid's dead yet."

Kettlebar swallowed. "What if he ain't?" he asked nervously.

"Do I have to draw you a picture?" Tiner growled. "See to it he *is* dead!"

"Tiner, you dirty son of a—" Service began.

"Shut up!" Tiner roared, cutting him off. "You're lucky you ain't got a belly full of lead. If I didn't want to stop another war from startin', I'd kill you where you stand. But don't try me too hard or I'll do it anyway."

That was when the rifle shot roared from the cave mouth, and Tiner's shifted gaze saw Jake Kettlebar stagger, then crash to one knee.

With a spasmodic motion, Tiner threw up his rifle and emptied it into the shadowy depths of the cave, his eyes like stone as the stock jolted against his shoulder.

There was no more firing from the rocks. Tiner shifted the Winchester to his left hand and slid the Colt from its holster before Service and Goodwill had moved another step. Pistol barrel pointed in their direction, Tiner looked down the gravel-scattered incline to where Kettlebar was struggling to his feet minus a bootheel.

"Missed for a change," Tiner muttered as Kettlebar

looked up toward him. "Well?" he said loudly to the hesitant cowhand.

"You want me to—"

"I said go get those pistols!" Tiner ordered the lopsided Kettlebar.

With a swallow, Kettlebar struggled down the incline like a man with a wooden leg, his eyes wide and anticipating on the silent mouth of the cave.

"Never mind lookin' in the rocks," Tiner called down.

A trembling breath emptied from Kettlebar. He hobbled quickly to the first pistol and picked it up.

"All right, get up here," Tiner commanded the two men. They trudged up the bank. "So you wouldn't listen to Thursday," Tiner said disgustedly. "Had to be brave little boys."

"Ya ain't gonna get away with this!" Service snapped.

"Shut up," Tiner said, turning and seeing that Kettlebar was scrambling up the bank and glancing over his shoulder as if he expected, at any second, to get a bullet in the back of his head.

"Take those two over to the camp," Tiner told the limping Kettlebar when he was over the ridge, the two pistols under his waistband. "Put 'em in a lariat circle, and if they try to leave it, kill 'em. Understand?"

Kettlebar nodded.

Tiner turned toward the two men. "All right," he said, "march. Unless you'd rather be dead heroes."

He stood there motionless awhile watching the three men walk slowly toward the camp, Service and Goodwill in the lead, Kettlebar limping behind, his rifle pointed at them.

"Heroes," Tiner muttered.

Then his lips pressed together and, turning, he looked across the stream to the pile of rocks where the boy was. He slid the Colt into its holster and leaned his empty rifle against one of the boulders near him.

Then he started down the incline slowly, heading straight for the cave. He'd had enough.

5

WHEN THE BLAST of shots first began, Jody's head faltered up sluggishly from the boulder and his heavy-lidded eyes fluttered open.

At first he was unable to focus on anything; the landscape blurred before him as if it were a layer of stony earth lying on the shifting surface of a lake. Heart pounding, Jody strained desperately to see. They were coming to get him; he knew it. He had to see so he could stop them.

The numb fingers of his left hand touched the rifle stock and tried to grip it. A frightened moan quavered in Jody's throat as the fingers failed to close. He reached across his body with his right hand and it threw him off balance; his left shoulder thudded against the hard ground.

A strangled gasp shook him. Agony was like the jab of a branding iron in his flesh, driving the dullness from his brain. He shoved up again, blinking away waves of dizziness, and looked across the boulder with wide, staring eyes.

Outside, the firing, after a momentary pause, had begun again, filling the sun-baked air with the whistle of slugs. After a moment of strained effort, Jody could see a flash of rifle fire between the two boulders where the Circle Seven man was.

Yet there were no bullets landing near the cave; Jody couldn't understand it. A dry rasping sounded in his throat as he swallowed. Who was the man firing at? Jody sat slumped against the boulder, staring dully across the way at the boulders with the blazing rifle poked between them.

Then a horseman galloped up on the other bank and, dropping down with his rifle, made a crouching run to the man behind the boulders. Jody shrank back unconsciously. It was the foreman of the Circle Seven.

A wave of pain from the wounded arm rushed across his brain, blacking him out for a moment. The landscape spun. Jody fell helplessly on his right side, gasping, struggling to remain conscious. The makeshift bandage around the arm had done little good. The wound plus his terrible thirst told Jody that he couldn't keep going much longer.

The shooting stopped. Jody lay panting in the silence, hearing again the torturing sound of the stream that was no more than ten strides away, the rushing current of cool, clear, fresh—

Someone yelled, "Get the hell out o' there!"

Then there was firing again; one shot, two, spaced apart by seconds. As quickly as possible, Jody pushed himself to a crouch and, blinking away the waves of darkness that rushed across him, he saw the foreman standing and firing a rifle—but still not at the cave.

Silence again; the foreman ordering, "Drop it!" to someone Jody couldn't see.

Then another jolt of pain in his arm. His head ached, felt as if it were expanding hotly, then contracting and clamping in his brain. Sight fled. A ragged sob broke in Jody's throat and he fought it off. Hand clutching at his wounded arm, he slumped forward against the boulder while, outside, the foreman ordered someone to cross the stream. Jody's eyes clouded.

He thought hours had passed when someone said, "Shut up," very loudly, and he struggled up again. He started, a bolt of breathless panic hitting him as he saw a strange man heading for the rocks.

Hand like lead, Jody reached into his holster and slid out the heavy Colt. He raised it unsteadily and tried to aim, but his target seemed to break apart and was obscured by fluttering curtains of darkness. Jody blinked hard, swallowed. The tense-faced man was closer now, approaching the cave with rifle extended in readiness.

Jody pulled the trigger, and the pistol jumped in his grip, the recoil knocking him on his back. Not a moment too soon, for in the next instant, the cave was a frenzy of ringing bullets. Jody heard them whining off rock and thudding into the earth around him. A streak of hot lead burned away skin on his right temple and made him twitch violently. Another slug scraped away boot leather.

Then the echoes of the rifle bursts had faded away across the prairie and the only sound was that of the stream and the distant bellow of startled cattle.

Until the man near the stream said, "You want me to—" and the foreman interrupted loudly: "I said go get those pistols!"

Jody pushed up again dizzily and squinted out at the sun-blazing area. He'd knocked off the man's bootheel, he saw. The man had trouble standing.

Nervously, Jody reached down for his pistol again, but then the foreman told the man to never mind about the rocks and Jody relaxed for a moment. He looked up at the two men being covered by the foreman's pistol. They were moving up the incline on the other side of the stream. One of them said something to the foreman, and the foreman told him to shut up.

Jody sat there breathing fitfully and watching the three men stand on the ridge waiting for the fourth to get back. He picked up his pistol and raised it shakily. A perfect target. If only he could see clearly. But no matter how he squinted or strained his eyes, the view was blurred and without substance. I have to try, he thought, dazed. He didn't know who the men were, but they were against the Circle Seven foreman. That was enough. He aimed as carefully as he could.

The hammer clicked loudly on an empty chamber.

Jody shuddered with alarm and thumbed back the hammer again, pulled the trigger. Another click.

Automatically, he tried to raise his left hand to break open the chamber, but it wouldn't come. Hot pain flooded his arm and shoulder, and the pistol barrel fell. It's empty, he thought—and there's no more.

When he could see again, he put down the pistol and broke open the chamber with his right hand. Empty. He reached for his Henry quickly, eyes searching up toward the ridge.

The foreman stood there alone, looking the other way. Jody felt his heartbeat grow heavy again, the increased flow of blood making his head pound.

The Henry was empty, too. Jody's mouth fell open and he jerked up his eyes again.

The foreman was starting down the bank toward him, his pistol holstered but with a look of expressionless menace on his face.

With a gasp, Jody threw himself on the saddlebags,

ignoring the jolt of pain and tore them open. He felt himself go limp with terror.

There was no more ammunition. Without realizing it, he'd fired it all.

His nostrils flared a moment, his teeth jammed together with a click. Jody Flanagan scuttled back into the shadows until his back was pressed against rock. The trembling fingers of his right hand dug into a pocket of his wool pants and closed over his jackknife. He didn't know what he meant to do with it, but he had to have something to fight with.

He opened the long blade with his teeth.

Breath shook his chest as he kept himself erect against the boulder despite pain and thirst and the welling threat of unconsciousness. The irregular opening to the cave seemed to waver before him. It fled away, then leapt back like a swallowing mouth. Jody wiped away sweat with the back of his right hand. The movement of his chest grew more agitated and his fingers became so tight on the knife that the blood was pressed from them.

The figure of the foreman appeared at the mouth of the cave.

Jody saw him crouch down, pistol in hand. Jody tried to hold his breath, tried to figure out what to do. Lunge toward the man? He'd be shot before he'd gone a step—even if he *could* lunge. Wait for the man to enter the cave? He knew the foreman wouldn't, and his throat drew taut.

Half-conscious rage blazed through him, and he braced himself against the wall for a fast start. At least he wouldn't die cringed against a wall like a frightened woman.

Outside, the foreman raised his pistol. "I'm countin' to three," he said.

6

AFTER THE TWO men had dwindled to specks in the distance, a grim-faced Mack Thursday eased his mount around and headed for his ranch.

He rode slowly, gazing straight ahead, his features molded to an expression of forced indifference. All right, if they wanted to kill themselves, that was their business. They didn't know, they just didn't *know*; not what a range war was like. Before they'd even come to the area, buffalo grass had overgrown the dozens of bleak, revealing mounds across the prairie—one of them belonging to the torn remnants of what had been his son.

Thursday's hands tightened on the reins. He wasn't going back and that was all there was to it. He wouldn't think about it anymore.

And why should they save this kid? he thought after a few moments. The kid had killed Circle Seven men. Tiner had a right to want his scalp. An eye for an eye. Through Thursday's mind filtered memories of the Bible stories his mother used to read when he was a boy. Daniel in the lion's den. Joseph and his brethren.

Jacob wrestling with an angel.

The angel represented doubt, his mother had told him. Thursday tried to push away the thought. It was something he didn't want to remember.

Tiner had a right to trap the boy. But the boy was only fighting for what was his. Men called this a free range; they expected it to be that way. A man had a right to refuse to pay crossing money. Tiner had no right to—

Tiner had a right—Tiner had no right. Was there a thing in life that wasn't mixed-up and twisted? What did a man decide? What was right and what was wrong?

If only it hadn't been a boy, a sixteen-year-old boy. Every time he thought of that boy, he saw his own son in those rocks, helpless. Tiner closing in.

Thursday pressed his lips into a bloodless line as though the effort would force back indecision. It wasn't his son; his son was dead and buried. He wasn't going to have a bloody range war on his conscience.

His chest rose and fell with heavy erratic breaths and the core of tension in him kept growing worse—like a watch spring being wound and wound.

Until the shots rang out in the distance and made him pull his mount around.

For a last uncertain moment, he held back the restless horse. Then with a jerk of his knees, he nudged it into a canter, then a gallop back toward the Circle Seven camp. He didn't know if he was doing wrong or right; he only knew he could not do otherwise. The loosening of tension in him told him so.

Decision made, his thoughts flew ahead to where the shots were being fired. What was happening? It sounded as if those two young fools had ridden straight into it without a plan in their hot heads. Thursday's lips twitched in a momentary grimace. I should have gone with them, he thought. There might have been a way.

Well, it was too late for that now. He spurred the horse into a faster gallop yet. Its hooves thundered across the hard-baked earth, and the wind was like an oven blast in Thursday's face. Far off, the shooting stopped, then started again.

Before he rode near enough to the rocks to be heard, Thursday reined his mount to the left and felt its jolting, sliding descent down the graveled incline beneath. The horse splashed across the river in a stride, over the cracked mud, and lunged up the opposite bank. There was a fringe of cottonwoods along that side, and the sound-carrying wind would be in his favor, too. He guided his mount along the ridge, eyes straining beneath the shadowing brim of his hat.

Far up the stream, he saw the small figures of two men walking across the water toward another man who had his rifle leveled at them. Thursday figured that the man with the rifle was probably Tiner. A fourth man was going past them, headed in the opposite direction.

Another shot rang out, this time from the rocks, and the Circle Seven man went down. The next second Tiner emptied his rifle into the rocks. Thursday wondered how well the boy was protected. He saw the man who had fallen down get up.

Then he saw Service's and Goodwill's horses grazing and, fearing that the hoofbeats of his mount might be heard despite the veiling of wind, he slowed the horse to a walk, then, after another sixty yards, dismounted and grounded the reins.

As he half ran, half walked across the hard ground, he could feel waves of heat billowing around him. He reached the end of the ridge and paused there a moment under the shade of a cottonwood, slipping a cartridge into the empty chamber of his Colt. Across the way only Tiner was left now, watching the three men move toward the Circle Seven camp.

Then Tiner turned around and started down the bank, headed for the rocks. Thursday's heartbeat jolted, and he skidded down the incline, losing balance and pushing himself up with his left hand on the burning hot stones. Shaking his hand, he hurried across the dusty dried mud and down along the stream edge so the sound of the current would cover his bootfalls.

Just as Tiner reached the mouth of what looked to Thursday like a natural cave, Thursday drew his pistol and stopped. He saw the foreman crouch before the cave, pistol in hand. Then Tiner stood up, raising his pistol.

"Tiner!"

The foreman's head snapped around, and his startled gaze jumped over to where the older man stood pointing a pistol at him. Then the surprised look was gone from Tiner's face and it was a death mask again. "You want your friends," he said, "they're in my camp."

Thursday shook his head.

"I said they're in my camp."

"I didn't come for them," Thursday told him.

"What then?"

"You know. Put down your pistol."

Only the tightening of skin across Tiner's cheeks indicated his rising temper. "You better go, Thursday."

"Tiner, I want that boy."

"You're not gettin' him," the foreman answered slowly.

Silence a moment, the two of them looking at each other cautiously.

Then Thursday spoke in a tired, regretful voice. "Then I guess that leaves us only one way."

The two shots came so close together that the three men in the camp thought it was one gun firing.

Bob Service's face twitched involuntarily as he stood there rigidly, ignoring the trickle of blood on his right arm, looking blankly toward the river.

Then, after a moment, breath emptied slowly from him. "There it is," he said, almost inaudibly.

John Goodwill, squatting beside him in the lariat circle, looked up, face still contorted from the pain of his wounded wrist. "We tried," he said without conviction.

"Sure," Service agreed bitterly, "we—"

Another shot exploded down by the river.

Service raged, "What the hell's he *doin'*? Cuttin' him to *pieces*?"

"Shut up," said Kettlebar, but there was no authority in his voice.

Suddenly very tired, Service hunkered down beside Goodwill. "One more notch for the Circle Seven," Service muttered in a tense, hating voice. Goodwill said nothing. Service went on, "While good old Mack Thursday rides away and saves the range."

"I said shut up," Kettlebar said.

Service ignored him.

Goodwill asked, "What d'ya think Tiner's gonna do with us?"

"I dunno," Service said in a lifeless voice. "I don't care." He felt like breaking something, fighting with his fists, anything to release the frustrated rage knifing through him.

"I guess he won't do nothin'," Goodwill said. "I guess he would've plugged us before if—" His voice broke off abruptly as he saw Service looking toward the river with an expression of amazement on his face. He turned his head suddenly and gasped.

"*God,*" he heard Kettlebar say in an incredulous voice.

Hobbling across the plain were two figures, one of them Mack Thursday. He limped heavily, a tense look of repressed pain on his face, his left arm around the waist of a young man.

Without a word, Bob Service bolted out of the lariat circle toward them.

"Hey, you—" Kettlebar shouted, then didn't finish. The rifle he raised to fire, he now lowered after an indecisive moment.

"Thursday!" Service greeted the older man as he ran up to him.

"Help the boy," Thursday gasped. "I'm all right."

Service put his arm around Jody Flanagan's waist. Relieved of the load, Mack Thursday limped on, his face set willfully as he fought down the pain of the slug in him. As Thursday limped into the camp, Kettlebar put down his rifle with a cautious movement.

"Go get your foreman," Thursday said.

"My—" Kettlebar stared at the older man as if he couldn't believe what he'd heard.

"Go on, go on," Thursday said irritably. Kettlebar turned without another word. "Goodwill, help him," Thursday said.

Still looking amazed, Goodwill started toward the river after the Circle Seven hand.

"Man, what *happened*?" Service asked excitedly after he'd put the boy down.

"Give him some water," Thursday told him as he slumped down on the ground with a wince. Service got Kettlebar's

canteen and handed it to the boy who, although he'd had
water from the stream, was still thirsty.

"Here, let me do that," Service said, moving quickly to
where Thursday was trying to wrap his bandanna around the
bleeding wound in his upper right leg.

"Tiner's dead?" Service asked, bandaging.

"I don't think so," the older man replied. "He can't last
long though."

Service nodded grimly. Then, aware of how he'd spoken
to Thursday that day, he looked down at the ground
awkwardly.

"Thursday, I . . ." Service began, and the older man
opened his eyes.

"What?" he said, glancing toward the boy. Before Service
could go on, Thursday asked the boy, "Feeling better?"

The boy nodded. "Yes, sir. Thanks a lot."

Thursday looked back to Service. "What is it?" he asked.

"I . . . I'm apologizin' for what I said to you before,"
Service told him.

Thursday shook it off. "Forget it." He closed his eyes.
Then, thinking of something, he opened his eyes again.
"Just remember one thing," he said, "there's more than one
reason for not fightin'."

7

THEY WERE ALL gone except for Thursday and Tiner. Service and Goodwill were taking the boy back to Thursday's ranch and, at the boy's insistence, the fifty cattle, too. Kettlebar had gone out to relieve the man on herd watch.

Tiner lay unconscious in the shade of an erected tarpaulin, his chest rising and falling in shallow, jerking movements. The dark red blotch on his chest bandage grew wider and wider.

Thursday sat near him, drinking a cup of water. He'd been thinking. All the time he'd ridden back, faced Tiner, fired on him, wounded him, gone to the boy, given him water, helped him over to the camp—all that time, he hadn't known why he was doing these things . . . not really, deeply.

Now he did. And he knew it wasn't because of his son. As a matter of fact, it was because of his son that he almost *hadn't* done it.

No, he'd done it because he'd realized, if not consciously, that a man had to settle each issue as it came up; he couldn't avoid the little battles without having to fight a bigger one

later on when all the small, unsettled battles added themselves up. A man had to settle each conflict when it
happened and at no other time; that was the way it had to go.
Progress came in little steps.

While he was thinking that, he noticed that Tiner's eyes
had opened.

"Drink?" he asked, and Tiner nodded once, weakly.

Thursday bent over him, but half the water ran from the
edges of the foreman's mouth. Thursday patted away the
heavy sweat on Tiner's immobile face.

"Th-thanks," Tiner muttered, a slow, rasping breath in his
throat as he looked up at the older man.

There was no talk of the shooting; that was done with,
accepted. Instead, Tiner said, "You'll be makin' some . . .
changes now." There was no angry regret or animosity in
his voice. He spoke a simple fact.

"There'll be changes," Thursday said quietly. "I'm stayin'
on here to see the start of it. To see your boys don't start up
another war."

Tiner nodded. "Yeah," he gasped, "another war . . .
wouldn't be . . . good." His head rolled to the side and he
stared up at the bright, blue sky. He knew, as Thursday did,
that when he was gone, the Circle Seven would lose its
dominance. Ralston would capitulate, the range would open
again.

Breath emptied from Tiner's lungs slowly until it seemed
as if he were completely drained of it. "Well," he mumbled,
swallowing, "I . . . did my job." He drew in a whistling
breath. "Can't . . . nobody say . . . different."

"You did your job," Thursday agreed.

Later, he pulled down the tarpaulin and drew it across the
still face of Rail Tiner. As he did, he noticed how the

foreman's hair ruffled slowly in the endless wind of the prairie.

Then, with a tired sigh, he sat down again and waited quietly for the men to come in from their day's work.

———◆———

TOO PROUD
TO LOSE

LEW TORRIN WOKE slowly that morning. His eyelids kept falling shut again and again before they finally stayed open.

Today. It was the first word that crawled across his sleep-thickened mind. Today he had to meet Frank Hamet, and one of them was going to die.

He turned his head on the pillow and looked out the window, mouth tightened. It was a bleak morning, gray and sunless. Even under the blankets he could almost feel the November frost that would make his blood run slow, deaden his reflexes. Lack of sunlight would hurt his vision . . . today, when his eyes would have to work perfectly or he'd die.

Die. He pushed away the thought and sat up quickly. A groan rumbled in his chest. A full night's sleep and still he was tired. He dropped his legs over the edge of the bed and sat staring at his veined hands, their backs almost bronze from the Arizona sun. He flexed the long fingers and tried to work limberness into them, but he couldn't. They were stiff; something was gone from them.

I'm forty, he thought, I can't expect to be the same.

His chest rose and sank heavily. That didn't change anything. He still had to meet Frank Hamet.

He reached out and picked up his watch from the bedside table. My God, he'd slept ten hours! Why hadn't Mary woken him?

The question was pointless; he already knew the answer. She'd let him sleep because she knew his exhaustion.

She didn't know about Hamet though—and she wouldn't know.

Lew Torrin still sat there, heavy-muscled shoulders limp, hands hanging slackly over his thighs. He wished he could lie down and sleep another ten hours. All the energy was gone from him. It was the way a man lived in this time: full grown at sixteen, burned-out at forty.

His gaze moved to the leather of his belt and holster hanging on the bedpost and settled on the worn handle of the Colt .44. Today that piece of apparatus would save his life or he would die.

It was unbelievable.

He stood up and lost himself in the activity of dressing, staring around the room to keep his mind from thinking. His eyes moved from the bowl and pitcher to the rumpled bed; to the carved chest at the door of the bed; to the hook rug Mary had made years ago; to their wedding picture on the wall; to the pictures of Lucy and Sarah taken in front of the tree last Christmas.

He kept looking at all of them while he pulled on his Levi's, buttoned up the flannel shirt, and sat on the bed to pull on stockings and boots.

Is that me? He couldn't help the question as he stared into the mirror at his dark blond hair graying at the temples, his tanned face creased from squinting and worrying. He ran his finger over the thin white scar on his temple still there from the fight.

He shook his head slowly as he drew the watch out of his shirt pocket after putting it in. Eleven. In two hours he had to meet Frank in the field behind the graveyard. His head kept shaking. It seemed impossible.

His mouth tensed. Well, it's *not*, he told himself angrily. That was the worst thing with being his age. It wasn't failing reflexes, or muscles that couldn't get enough rest, or even fear. It was this endless thinking that made things so hard.

He pinned on his badge before the mirror, looking at its dull burnished glitter. Sheriff of Dannerville for twenty years and nothing to show for it but this little piece of metal on his chest. Why did a man do it? Why did he devote himself to keeping the law in a town, following the steps of his father and his father's father?

For the life of him, he didn't know.

Torrin grabbed his gun belt and dragged it up over the bedpost. He walked quickly across the shadowed room, his boots clumping on the floorboards. Don't start thinking, he told himself. It's better not to think. Go into it blindly, thoughtlessly. It was simple, really. Twenty years of keeping law, that didn't matter. Eighteen years of marriage, that counted for nothing. There were only two things—living and dying.

He came slowly down the stairs, the smell of hotcakes and bacon and strong coffee floating up to him. As he descended, he felt the heaviness of his body bearing down on one leg, then the other. He felt the weight of the pistol belt dragging on his arm. He heard the measured ticking of the clock as he moved past it and saw, from the corners of his eyes, the sluggish arcing of its pendulum. He heard his boot heels thumping on the stairs and saw the dull glow of the polished banister. The heavy panels of the front door, the clothes tree with his hat and leather jacket on it. Everything—all the things of his house, of his life, that might, in two hours, be suddenly ended in a wash of agonized blackness.

Don't think! The words exploded in his mind. But then he heard the sound of Mary's feet moving with quick precision in the kitchen and everything welled over him again—all the inconceivable details massing against the black backdrop of dying.

She looked up from the stove. "Good morning, dear," she said.

He tried to smile but couldn't manage more than a stiff twitching at the corners of his mouth.

Her face grew sympathetic. "Still tired?" she asked.

"No, I feel better," he said.

"Good. Sit down now. I'll get your breakfast."

He moved to the chair and slung the gun belt over one of the back posts. No, I won't tell her, he thought, feeling a sudden churning in his stomach as he realized he wanted desperately to tell her about it.

He sank down in the chair and clenched tight fists under the table where she couldn't see.

"You shouldn't have let me sleep so long," he said.

"You needed it," she told him. "Jake can handle the office for one morning."

Lew stared at the clean dishes before him, the coffee mug, the silverware. This will be the last food I eat, the thought came, and he tightened angrily at the cruelty of his own mind.

"The girls gone?" he asked quickly, hoping to drown away thought with words.

"Been in school since nine," she said easily, coming over to get his plate.

He caught her hand impulsively and she looked down at him, a spark of surprise in her eyes.

He forced a smile. "Thanks for . . . letting me sleep," he said.

"I wish you could sleep all day," she said.

Then she went to the stove and his hand dropped back. So do I, he thought, so do I wish I could sleep all day.

Suddenly his hands clenched into bloodless fists on his lap and he wanted to cry out, No! No, it isn't fair! Why should I throw my life away for some hellion who never did a decent thing in his life?

"Are you cold, Lew?" she asked as she brought the food to him.

He swallowed hard. "A little," he said. "Looks like it's getting ready to snow."

"Pretty soon now," she said and put down his plate.

"Looks fine," he said and smiled up at her.

"I'll get your coffee," she said, and his fingers twitched impotently in his lap as he fought off the impulse to grab her hand again. He drew in a shaking breath and braced himself. That's enough, he ordered himself. That's enough.

While he ate slowly, he tried not to think, but he kept thinking about Frank Hamet.

Lew had known Frank's father. He'd seen old Joshua Hamet killed by a runaway horse, been a pallbearer at the funeral, taken up the collection that helped the Widow Hamet start the small dry goods shop that provided her income.

And he'd seen Frank grow from a pampered baby to a brat flinging stones at passing horses, playing hooky from school. He'd seen Frank grow into a lean adolescent who started drinking and gambling too soon and took up with the wrong kind of friends.

And now this same Frank Hamet had challenged him and would be waiting in a field to kill him.

"Aren't you hungry, Lew?"

Mary's question made him look up with a startled expression on his face.

"Aren't you feeling well?" she asked.

"No, I'm just . . . oh, I don't know." He managed a grin. "Guess I'm not used to so much sleep. I'm still groggy."

"Why don't you stay home today and let Jake handle things?"

"No, I—"

"There's nothing important to do is there?"

"No. But—"

She smiled gently. "All right, dear. But please take it easy."

He lowered his head so she wouldn't see him swallow. "I will," he said.

He finished the coffee and stood up, hands trembling a little as he buckled on the gun belt that seemed to weigh a hundred pounds. Then he drew out his watch. Eleven-thirty. He leaned over and kissed Mary's cheek. "I'm going," he said, feeling something cold in his stomach.

She put her hands on his arms. "Don't work too hard now," she said. "*Please*. And come home early for dinner."

He looked at her another moment, trying to print her face in his mind: the curl hanging loosely across her right temple, the soft brown eyes, the glowing cheeks, the warm full lips which he kissed now, feeling her body against his.

"See you at dinner," she said softly.

"Good-bye," he answered.

He could hardly feel his legs as he walked across the

kitchen. I'm leaving her, he thought. I'm leaving my wife and I'll never see her again. He kept his lips pressed together to hold back the sound he felt pushing up in his throat, and his body felt like a block of stone.

Then he was in the hall, putting on his jacket and hat, hardly conscious of his body, he was so numb with dread. Not for his life, but that he would never see Mary or the girls again. He actually took a step back toward the kitchen, meaning to go in and tell her and plan out what she should do if he didn't come back.

But he checked himself and stood there buttoning up his jacket, face a mask of resolution. He wasn't going to tell her. He didn't want her to go through what he was going through.

Before he went out, he looked around the hall and knew, in that moment, how very much he loved this house because, in it, had been all the happiness of his life. The bringing home of his bride, the years of domestic pleasures, the births of Lucy and Sarah; all the thousand little things that added up to the total of a man's existence.

At one o'clock they might all be ended.

He went out quickly into the cold, frost-edged air and walked down the path, shutting the gate behind him, then plunging his hands into his jacket pockets again. Every jolting bootfall was like a blow against his heart, and he didn't dare look back.

"Hello, Sheriff!"

He heard a thin voice call out and, turning his head, saw five-year-old Mickey Porter playing in his front yard. He smiled with effort and waved to Mickey. A son, the thought came without warning, that's the worst part.

He realized then that he'd avoided that thought most of all. He felt that it was arrogance on his part to feel so strongly about the continuation of his line. It's something I was taught, he reasoned with himself. My grandfather told my father and my father told me. Torrin means law in Dannerville. That was it, a slogan, a saying that you learned by rote as if it were a law of the universe. Torrin means justice, means law.

Torrin meant Torrin—that was all it meant. Lew felt it strongly. The line would end and nothing would be lost by it. The world would go on, children being born and old men dying, and Torrin would become a forgotten name; the dust-heavy title of an ancient strain who tried to keep the law in a little Arizona town and finally passed from being.

He was so lost in thought he almost rammed into the Widow Hamet

"Sheriff Torrin," she said, looking up at him as he towered over her.

Automatically, he caught the brim of his hat between two fingers and drew it off, his gray-tinged blond hair ruffling in the wind.

"Please, put your hat on," the Widow Hamet said in her thin voice. "It's much too cold."

He smiled politely and put his hat back on. "You . . . want to see me?" he asked.

"Yes," she answered. "Deputy Catwell told me you were still at home."

He nodded, feeling himself tighten. This was only stalling, he knew, only words that would lead to other words, words he didn't want to hear.

"Sheriff, I know I have no right to come to you like this," she said.

"Of course you do," he said, not wanting to say it. "You're an old friend."

She tried to smile but couldn't. "I mean, I know it's

Frank's fault. I—can't defend him, Sheriff, I know it's his fault. But—"

He didn't say anything. He looked down at her, feeling empty.

She drew in a quick breath. "Isn't there any way?" she asked.

He felt himself stiffen with anger that Frank had told his mother and driven one more knife into her already wounded heart.

"I'm sorry you know about it," he said, knowing it wasn't the answer she wanted.

"Sheriff Torrin, I *tried*," she said, her eyes pleading with him. "I begged him not to do the terrible things he's done. I begged him not to fight with you. I know there are no arguments for him but . . ." Her voice broke. "He's my boy," she said. "Don't hurt him, Sheriff. Don't hurt my boy!"

He stood there numbly, staring down at her as though from a great height. Then he heard a voice speaking and knew it was his own but didn't know where the words came from.

"I'm sorry, Missus Hamet," he said. "I can't stop the fight now. I would if I could, but I'm helpless. It's gone too far. Unless Frank backs out, I can't do anything. I'm sheriff, and I have to go through with it."

He wondered what had happened to the Widow Hamet, and it wasn't until he'd walked thirty feet that he realized he'd stepped past her quickly and walked away without another word.

He strode past Martin's gunsmith shop, past the saddlery, the feed store. He walked past people and knew what they were thinking. He said good morning to no one. His face was expressionless as he walked steadily toward the jail. Far off, he heard the church bell toll noon. In an hour, he thought. An hour.

He tried to regain the strength-giving rage he'd felt a few moments before by thinking of all the things Frank Hamet had done.

The day had come when shooting roared in the Lazy Wheel Saloon, and he had run there to find Frank in a drunken rage, firing his pistol while friends watched approvingly.

He'd taken away Frank's pistol, dragged him from the saloon, and tossed him into jail. And Frank, shamed in the eyes of his friends, had screamed at him, face mottled with fury, the cords in his neck standing out.

"I'll kill you for this, Torrin! I swear to God, I'll kill you!"

He hadn't believed Frank. He'd turned away from the abusive cursing and left him there for twenty-four hours. And when he'd released him, Frank had said nothing.

The jail was locked. Lew let himself in and walked across the room, listening to the faint crackling of flames inside the wood stove. Sinking down wearily before his desk, he leaned back and looked up at the clock pendulum moving from side to side in rhythm with the ticking. It's my life, he thought, ticking away while I sit here.

It had begun soon after the jailing incident. Wherever Lew rode or walked he would, seemingly by accident, come across Frank. Frank would never look at him. He'd be sitting in front of his mother's shop, or in front of the hotel or the saloon, or standing by a hitching rack, or sitting in back of the saloon—examining his pistol.

That went on for weeks.

Then came the drawing and the firing. Whenever Lew

rode outside of town he'd come across Frank practicing. Frank would draw and fire at something, very quick and sure; more so with each passing week.

And that was all. Never an overt move, never anything that could possibly be interpreted as a challenge. Only this carefully planned and executed intimidation. Months passing and Lew's nerves getting tighter and tighter because he knew just what Frank was doing and had no power to stop it.

It got to the point where he actually found himself taking extra rides outside of town in order to practice drawing and firing.

Then a reaction set in and he stopped, feeling like a fool for doing it in the first place. And, trying to pretend he felt nothing, he'd gone on about his business, every day watching Frank get faster and knowing that, one day, Frank would know himself fast enough.

The day had come. But still there was nothing overt.

Frank started grinning at him.

That was all—just grinning. At first Lew thought it would be easy to ignore, but when the whole town started watching, it began to tell on his nerves. Frank seemed to devote his time to plaguing Lew with grins and then, little by little, with carefully measured insults spoken behind his back which, sooner or later, reached Lew's ears.

Until finally, one day—a day of frustrating irritations—Frank had snickered as Lew passed in the street and Lew, goaded to sudden fury, had whirled on him and knocked him into the street. There had been the fight—a clawing, kicking, frothing Frank against him. And when the fight had ended, a beaten Frank had flung his challenge and everything was crystallized into a simple alternative: life or death.

Lew Torrin's eyes refocused on the pistol in his lap and,

suddenly, he jerked his finger out of the trigger guard and thumped the pistol down on the desk.

He sat there wondering if he should write a letter to Mary. His will had been made years before; it rested safe in the bank vault. But shouldn't he write a letter now to let her know how he felt?

He picked up a pen and ran its dry, ink-black tip across the back of his hand. Dear Mary—words ran through his mind—I'm writing to you because, in forty minutes, I'll be dead . . .

The door opened and Jake Catwell came in. "Mornin', Lew," he said.

Lew nodded, then felt himself tighten as Jake glanced up at the wall clock. For a moment he became afraid that the fight was so widely known Mary might hear of it.

"Everything all right?" he asked Jake.

"Sure," Jake said. "Fine."

Lew nodded again and took some papers from the top drawer so he'd have something to look at beside his hands and the pistol on the desk. Jake slung off his mackinaw and tossed it on the bench.

"Cold as hell out," he said. "Probably snow today."

Lew didn't answer. He was suddenly conscious of the fact that he was still wearing his leather jacket in the warmth of the room.

"Let Melter out," he said abruptly.

"Thought we was keepin' him two days."

"No, let him out. Tell him to go home and stop drinking."

Jake snickered as he headed for the cells. "That'll be the day," he said.

Lew sat there and heard the muffled voices of Jake and Sam Melter in the back. He thought of how simple this whole situation would have been for his father, because his father had lived in a time when a man never got a chance to slow down and worry. There were more than drunks to put in jail then, civic picnics to police, petty merchant's squabbles to settle, fights to referee or end. In those days there were murders and robberies and endless gunplays to keep a man at a keen edge of readiness.

Not now.

Jake came back in. "Go see if the stage is in," Lew told him. "Expecting some posters."

"Ain't due in for half hour yet, Lew."

"It might be early."

"Never is."

"Will you do what I say!"

Jake looked at him a moment, then shrugged once. "Okay, Lew," he said, putting on his mackinaw again. He walked to the door, then turned. "Good luck, Lew," he said.

Lew kept his head down, and when the door shut, he felt the rush of cold wind across his hands and face.

He looked up at the clock again. Almost twelve-thirty. In fifteen minutes he'd walk over to the stable. He could start now and walk to the graveyard, but he didn't want to do that; he'd get too tired. No, the thought came, I'll ride to the graveyard.

He almost ran right into Mary as he went out.

She threw herself against him, her face twisted with terrible fright, her hands clutching at his arms.

"Lew!" she gasped. "Why didn't you tell me?"

His stomach muscles jerked in as he looked at her flushed face. She had only a thin shawl over her dress. "Mary," he said confusedly, "what are you—"

"How could you go without telling me?" she asked.

He swallowed. "Who told you?" he asked.

"Frank's mother," she said quickly. "Lew, you're not really—"

"Come in, Mary, come in; you'll catch your death of cold standing out here."

"But—"

"Come *in*." He led her into the warmth of the jail and sat her down at his desk.

"There," he said. "Wait for me here. I have to go."

"Lew, you're not going to—"

"Mary, please," he begged. "This is my job. I have to do it, can't you see that?"

She sat wordlessly, staring up at him as he took out his watch and looked at it. A quarter to one. "I have to go," he said again.

"Lew, please," she started. "You—" She stopped and lowered her head with a sob. "You should have told me," she said brokenly. "Why didn't you tell me?"

His hands closed into fists, and he stood there staring down at her helplessly, thinking, I've got to get out of here. I've got to get out of here.

"It's all right," he said huskily. "I'll . . . come back."

She was up and in his arms then, shaking terribly. He kept patting her back with numb fingers and staring at the wall clock. One o'clock, I have to be there at one o'clock, he thought.

He kissed her cold cheek then and turned quickly. "Good-bye," he said, and he felt her watching him as he walked out of the jail into the cold November afternoon.

He walked quickly to the stable, not sure of what he felt at that moment. It wasn't fear, he knew, but it wasn't strength either. It was more a sense of complete inevitability.

No, he wouldn't think about it. He hunched his shoulders forward and rode slowly down the street, head lowered to keep the wind from his face. He could feel it buffeting coldly against him as he watched thin wisps of his horse's steaming breath.

Then, suddenly, without knowing why, he lifted his head and squared his shoulders. He looked straight ahead into the wind, noticing from the corners of his eyes how people watched him as he rode by. Remember me like this, he thought, proud and unafraid.

At two minutes to one, he reined up at the edge of the graveyard and tied his horse to the picket fence. For a moment, he stood there patting his horse's crest. Then, abruptly, he unbuttoned his jacket and slung it over the pommel, pulled out his pistol and checked it, then replaced it, satisfied.

He was ready.

He pushed through the gate and started across the deserted graveyard. Far out in the field, he saw a cluster of waiting men. He walked faster, anxious to be there and get it over with. He heard his boots crunching down the stiff grass as he threaded a path among the tombstones, eyes directed at the slender figure standing in the middle of the field, waiting, right hand on pistol butt, right arm cocked out languidly.

His mouth tightened. Be cute, he thought, be as cute as you like, little boy—I'll end your cuteness if it kills me. At his sides, his hands grew rigid. He hardly felt the cold.

He reached the edge of the field and entered, and all the men stopped talking abruptly and looked at him with the withdrawn curiosity of watchers at a killing. Feeling nothing, Lew Torrin looked around from man to man, avoiding until last the tight face of Frank Hamet, thirty yards away.

As their eyes met, Frank's hand left his pistol butt and fell to his side. Lew felt his arm muscles tighten in readiness.

Then, abruptly, he let his gaze drop. Slowly, almost lethargically, he took out his watch, pushed in the catch, and saw the front cover spring open.

Still twenty seconds to go. He stood there, head down, watching the second hand. Let him wait, he thought, amazed at his own calm, let him wait for me. He said one o'clock. One o'clock it would be.

Fifteen seconds, fourteen, thirteen. Lew Torrin stood erectly, not even glancing up at Frank Hamet. Eleven, ten, nine . . .

The sudden explosion tore open the stillness, and Lew saw the dirt at his feet kick up with a black spouting. His eyes jerked up in shocked surprise, and he saw the pistol in Frank's hand and heard the second shot.

Instinctively, he jumped to the side, but the bullet tore up the ground a yard in front of him.

A sudden fire sparked in Lew's brain. He's afraid! he thought in startled wonder.

The third shot came closer but still only blew up a spurt of earth that spattered across his Levi's and boots. And, suddenly, a broad smile appeared on Torrin's face. He couldn't help it.

Almost casually, he clicked shut the watch cover and slid it into his pocket. He saw Frank's face twist and heard the strangled curse flung across the field. Then Frank extended his arm and Lew could actually see the pistol barrel shake as Frank tried to aim.

Without even thinking, Lew dropped his arm, drew the pistol smoothly from his holster, and fired.

Frank cried out hoarsely as the pistol flew from his hand and skidded across the hard dirt. He clutched at his wrist and stared at Lew, a flickering of terror in his dark eyes. Lew started toward him and Frank backed off.

"No," he said. "Don't, Sheriff. Don't kill me!"

But Lew had holstered his gun even before he reached the boy. He walked up to where Frank stood and, grabbing him by his right arm, he drove the back of his free hand sharply across Frank's mouth.

Frank cried out and stumbled back, tripping and slipping to one knee. Lew looked down into the white, contorted face of the young man who had made this day a horror for him. And suddenly all the anger left him completely.

"Go home and get your things," he said flatly. "You have till five o'clock to get out of town. You hear me?"

"Yeah. Yeah, I hear you," Frank said.

"If you're still here at sunset, I'll kill you."

He couldn't help the pleasure he felt at the look of complete terror on Frank's face. I've got it coming to me, he thought.

He stood in the field a long time, watching Frank hurry across the graveyard, and he felt a wonderful, warming relaxation as if, finally, he'd gotten the rest he had needed for so long.

He sighed and bent over to pick up the fallen pistol. As he stuck it under his belt, he looked around. "All right," he said, without anger, "get out of here; the show's over."

When all the men had gone, he took out his watch.

Ten minutes after one. He shook his head. Three hours of agony for ten minutes of victory. He smiled to himself. Well, it seemed odd, but it was worth it.

As he started for his horse he felt a rich, healthy hunger in himself and knew he wanted a walloping dinner.

As he mounted, snow began to fall, the whiteness of it like a clean robe across his town.

LITTLE JACK CORNERED

SHORTLY AFTER DARK that night, two men pushed in through the slatted doors of the Latigo Saloon and stopped in their tracks. Behind them, the doors flapped back and forth, squeaking on hinges in need of oil. It was the only sound.

"Where *is* everybody?" asked Haskell.

"Dunno," the big man answered. He stood there tentatively, broad hands thumb-hooked over his belt while Haskell walked to the bar, stepped up on the foot rail, and looked behind the counter. He turned back to Melton and shrugged.

Then Kelly, the bartender, came out of the back room carrying two empty bourbon bottles. When he saw the two men, he twitched and jerked back a glance over his right shoulder. He started toward them, tiptoeing in gingerly haste.

"Hey, what's—" Haskell said before the bartender grimaced and gestured violently with his free arm.

"What's wrong?" Haskell asked when Kelly had reached them.

"Keep it down," cautioned the bartender, throwing back

another glance. "You boys better drag it. Jed Baladine's back there."

"*Baladine.*" Melton whistled softly through his teeth. "That's why them folks in the street was starin' at us when we come in."

"What's he doin' here?" asked Haskell, looking toward the back room.

Kelly swallowed and licked his lips nervously, another automatic glance twisting his head around.

"His brother Artie got the rope yesterday over Hubbard City," he said. "Now, come on boys, get out o' here. He's got three bottles o' hell in his gut and he's shootin' mean."

"His kid brother with 'im?" Haskell asked.

"*No.* Now, will ya go?"

"Yeah, let's go, Little Jack," said Melton. "We don't want no trouble."

"Who's gonna make trouble?" Haskell asked irritably. "We come—"

"Will ya keep it *down*?" whispered Kelly.

"Listen, I come twenny-three miles for a drink and I'm gonna have one," said Haskell.

Kelly gritted his teeth. "If I sell ya a bottle, will ya hightail it then?" he asked.

"What've ya got your back up for?" Haskell asked. "We ain't fixin' to bother him none."

The bartender closed his eyes for a few seconds, then opened them on Melton's broad face. "Look, will ya get your friend out o' here," he said, "before he gets blowed apart?"

Melton said, "Come *on*, Little Jack."

"Oh . . . get us a bottle then," Haskell said disgustedly. He tugged up angrily at his gun belt. "Man can't even . . ."

Kelly turned and hurried for the bar.

"I wonder where the sheriff is," Melton whispered, looking warily toward the back room.

"Home hidin' in bed most likely," Haskell said.

"That's where *I'd* be if I was him," the big man said. "That's better'n gettin' blowed full o' holes by Baladine."

Haskell made a scoffing sound and turned away. The two men stood waiting while Kelly grabbed a bottle of bourbon from the shelf and started back. In the back room they heard a cough.

"Don't see why we should have to . . ." Haskell let another mutter drag into silence.

Kelly reached them and slapped the bottle into Haskell's hand.

"How much?" Haskell asked.

"Nothin'. Just clear out o' here before—"

"Where's my bottle?"

Kelly whirled and the three men stared at the giant figure of Jed Baladine standing in the back doorway.

His dark clothes were soiled and wrinkled, his high-top boots filmed with dust. Two long Colts dragged their belts and holsters well below his hips. He wore his dark hat level, the brim shading his mottled, bearded face. The ends of his drooping mustache dripped whiskey.

"Who're you?" he asked thickly, glazed eyes moving over Haskell and Melton.

"The boys was just leavin'," said Kelly, straining out a smile. "Just bought them a bottle and—"

"They ain't leavin'," said Baladine. His tongue labored at his upper lip. "They ain't leavin' till I say so."

"Sure, Mr. Baladine," Kelly answered in a faint, hollow voice.

Baladine lurched from the doorway and moved in short,

listing strides to the bar. He fell against it and stood there, leaning.

"Bottle," he slurred.

"Right away," Kelly said, hustling for the bar.

"What do we do?" Melton whispered aside.

Haskell shrugged, slouched there, the bottle dangling from his left hand. At the bar, Baladine pulled another bottle away from Kelly and tilted it, the honey-colored bourbon splashing up the sides of the glass and splattering across the dark wood of the bar. Baladine put down the bottle and tossed the whiskey into his mouth. Part of it ran soaking into his mustache and down his chin.

"Well, I guess we'll be moseying," Haskell said while the outlaw was pouring himself a third drink. Melton threw a startled glance at his friend. Neither of them moved.

Baladine turned his head slowly and looked over, his pale blue eyes slitted, crow's-feet cutting into puffy flesh, his yellow-toothed mouth sagging open.

"*I said stay,*" he said.

Haskell swallowed dryly. "Why?" he asked, trying to sound casual.

"*Little Jack*—" Melton started, then shut up as Baladine pushed away from the bar and stood waveringly.

"Come 'ere," he said to Haskell.

"Mister, we don't want no trouble," Melton said quickly. There were worry lines around his mouth like white scars in copper-colored stone.

The outlaw's gaze slid over to Melton.

"Where's your pistol, cow boy?" he asked.

Melton licked at drying lips. "I . . . don't pack one," he said.

Baladine grunted. "Yella snake," he said. He leaned

against the bar again and looked back at Haskell. "I said come 'ere," he said.

Haskell's lips stirred as though he were about to argue. Then his throat stirred and he walked over to where Baladine was while the other two men watched motionlessly.

"You got a pistol," Baladine said.

Haskell swallowed, head dipping once. "Yeah," he said faintly.

"Know how t'use it?" Baladine asked.

"Wh-why?"

"Ya know how t'use it?"

Haskell swallowed quickly. "Some," he said.

The dark tip of Baladine's tongue slid out between his lips and curled up against his mustache. He made an amused sound, and the tongue slid back into his mouth.

"Some," he said. His broad chest twitched with a coughing chuckle. "Little Jack," he said, snickering. "Why d'they call ya Little Jack, I wonder."

Haskell's lips strained into a conciliatory smile.

"Well, both my pal 'n' me's named Jack," he said. "He's bigger'n me so . . ." He shrugged, then impulsively put his bottle on the bar top. "Here, ya want this?" he asked.

Baladine kept looking at him, face a flat, sour mask under his hat brim.

"I don' like Little Jacks," he said. "What d'ya think o' that?"

Haskell's lips twitched. He started to say something, but it died in his throat. His laugh was a nervous flutter of sound.

"Ya think that's funny?" Baladine asked.

Haskell cleared his throat. "No," he said. "I—"

137

"Mr. Baladine, we—" Kelly began, then pressed his lips together suddenly as the tall outlaw looked at him.

Baladine looked back at Haskell. "Make ya a bet, *Little* Jack," he said, smiling mirthlessly.

Haskell tried to smile back but couldn't. "W-what about?" he asked.

Baladine spat into the gaboon, looked up.

"I bet ya twenny dollars," he said, "I can kill somebody 'fore you can." His eyes were stone.

Little Jack gestured feebly. "I . . . well, sure ya can," he said. "You can shoot better'n me any day."

Baladine stood away from the counter. "Put your money on the bar," he said.

"But I—"

"Put your money on the bar."

"I ain't *got* no twenny dollars."

"Put what ya got on the bar," Baladine said.

"Mister, we don't want no trouble," Melton said.

Baladine looked over at him, jaw sagging. "I don' wanna hear no more from you," he said, "unnerstand, yella poke?"

Melton bit his lip and didn't answer.

Little Jack was fingering at the pockets of his flannel shirt. "*Get it out!*" Baladine said. Haskell emptied the pockets with shaking fingers and put everything on the bar. Baladine looked at it, then shoved a hand into his trouser pocket and spilled silver coins across Little Jack's belongings.

"There," he said. A deep chuckle sounded in his chest and he leaned forward. "Ya know why I'm gonna win?" he asked. "Ya know why, *Little* Jack?"

Haskell looked at him blankly.

"*Do* ya?" Baladine demanded.

"No, sir," Haskell answered.

Baladine smiled. "I'm gonna win 'cause I'm gonna kill *you*," he said.

"*What?*"

Baladine's chest lurched with soundless laughter. He shook his head. "You dumb little Jack," he said.

"Wait a minute, m-mister," said Haskell, "I ain't got no fight with you."

He started violently as Baladine stepped back and raised his hands.

"Go ahead," said Baladine. "You draw first—*Little* Jack."

"Wait a minute, will ya?" Haskell asked in a thin, shaky voice. "I ain't got no fight with you. *Wait!*"

He shrank back as Baladine drew swiftly, then stood trembling as the outlaw laid his pistols on the bar.

"There," said Baladine, chuckling. "There." He stepped away from the counter. "Now go ahead, *Little* Jack. Go ahead." He stood smiling and waiting.

"But I ain't—"

"*Fill your hand, boy,*" Baladine said in a low, warning voice. "I'm countin' t'three."

"Will ya wait a minute!" Jack said.

"One," said Baladine.

"Mister, we don't want no—" Melton started.

"Two," said Baladine.

Little Jack went rigid, his face drawn flat and smooth.

"*Three!*" Baladine lunged for his gun. It was in his hand before Little Jack's pistol was halfway from its holster. Baladine thumbed back the hammer and fired.

There was a clicking sound in the silence. Then the room shook with the blast of Little Jack's .45 and Baladine jolted violently as the slug hit. For a moment, he stood looking dumbfounded at Jack. Then his free hand rubbed across his shirtfront and he stared down blankly at the blood-smeared fingers.

"*You son of a bitch,*" he gasped as he fell against the bar and slid down into a heap.

There was a moment of wordless suspension, the only sound in the room a resonant ticking of the wall clock while the three men gaped at the sprawled outlaw.

Then Kelly muttered, "Holly . . . jumpin' . . ." and Little Jack winced as smoke from his Colt curled acridly into his nostrils. With a jerking motion, he shoved the pistol back into its holster and pulled his hand off the butt as if it were burning him.

"He's *dead*?" Melton asked in an unbelieving voice.

Kelly circled the bar and squatted by the outlaw, feeling for a heartbeat. He lifted a blank gaze and nodded twice.

"*Holy* . . ." Melton hurried over and looked at Baladine, then at Haskell. "*Little Jack,*" he said.

Haskell swallowed. "I . . ." Breath faltered from his lips as he stared at Baladine. "I didn't . . ." he started again, then couldn't finish.

Suddenly, Kelly was on his feet, dark shoes thumping as he ran for the batwing doors. A startled Little Jack and Melton watched him go. Outside, they heard him shout, "Baladine's dead!"

Little Jack shuddered. "What's he *tellin'* everybody for?" he said angrily. Melton shook his head, his gaze still moving from Baladine to his friend and back again. Little Jack turned away suddenly and reached for a bottle of whiskey.

The men came. Slowly at first, pushing open the doors and peering in over each other's shoulders with the half-awed, half-excited look of men about to witness something interestingly gruesome. When they saw Baladine lying on the floor, they pushed in like curious boys, then edged in slowly until they had formed a loose semicircle around the body, whistling softly, commenting in murmurs. Little Jack stood restively, drinking. He half turned to look at the men, then couldn't turn back.

In a moment, a stout, gray-haired man stepped forward and said, "Thank you, boy," and shook Little Jack's hand. "He was a man needed killing."

"Well, it was only a—" Little Jack started to say, but the rest of the men, the ice broken, swarmed around him enthusiastically, slapping him on the shoulders and back, shaking his hand and congratulating him. "It was only an accident," he kept telling them, but they wouldn't listen They laughed and bought drinks and stared at Baladine and toasted, "Here's to Little Jack Haskell. Here's *to* ya, boy!"

Jack stood in their midst, trying to smile. "It was only an accident," he said, but his voice was drowned out. He kept drinking and avoiding the eyes of Melton and the bartender. He drank and didn't look at Baladine.

"Good center shot," said the sheriff when he arrived with the undertaker. "You got a ree-ward comin', son."

"Well . . ." said Little Jack.

"How'd it happen?" the sheriff asked, smiling amiably because Baladine would not trouble his office any longer.

Twenty-year-old Little Jack stood against the bar, feeling everyone's admiring and half-fearing eyes on him. He licked his lips.

"Well, he picked a fight," he said, "and . . . well, he put his pistols on the bar and counted up t'three and . . ." He swallowed and shrugged, not looking at Melton who was standing nearby. "And . . ."

"Hurray fer Little Jack!" cried a man near the door, and Haskell didn't say any more.

Later, Melton and he rode back to the ranch they worked

on. Nothing was said until they were almost there. Then Melton said, "That was a lucky thing happened, Little Jack, Baladine's gun jammin' like that."

Haskell gritted his teeth and only grunted.

"Guess they . . . all think you . . ." Melton started.

"Look, I told 'em, didn't I?" Haskell broke in. "*You* heard me."

Melton nodded once. "Guess it didn't do much good," he said.

Little Jack blew out heavy breath. "Well, I *told* 'em," he muttered.

"What about the sheriff?"

"What about 'im?" Little Jack snapped.

The big man looked over at Haskell, who was hunched stiffly in his saddle.

"Nothin', I guess," he said.

They were unsaddling beside the corral when Melton said, "Wonder what his kid brother'll do."

Little Jack's hands froze on the hind cinch and he looked aside suddenly at his friend. "*What?*" he asked faintly.

"His kid brother," Melton said, "Kirk Baladine."

Little Jack had clean forgotten about that.

Melton stopped in the shadow of a cottonwood tree and leaned forward, squinting at the moonlit figure standing by the stream, drawing and redrawing as fast as he could. A cool night wind ruffled Little Jack's sandy hair as he stood, legs braced apart, snatching out his Colt, thumbing back the hammer and pulling the trigger. Melton heard the hammer clicking against each empty chamber rim.

The big man stood there a few minutes watching in silence. Then, clearing his throat conspicuously, he started down the soft, sloping ground, the heels of his boots sinking in as he walked. By the time he reached Haskell, the pistol was holstered and Little Jack was hunkered down, looking out casually over the drought-narrowed stream.

"What ya doin' up?" Melton asked.

Little Jack shrugged mechanically. "Didn't feel like sleepin'," he said.

Melton was about to say something about Little Jack wearing the gun, then decided against it. He yawned and stretched his long, beefy arms.

"What'd the sheriff say t'day?" he asked, trying to sound only mildly interested.

Little Jack cleared his throat. "Nothin'," he said. "Just give me the money is all."

"Oh." Melton looked at the tense, chalky, moonlit face of his friend. "He didn't . . . say nothin' about—"

"Why *should* he?" Little Jack said heatedly.

Melton shook his head and stood there a little while longer, thumbs hooked over the tops of his wool pants.

"What're *you* up for?" Little Jack asked.

Melton grunted. "Nothin', I guess. I . . . heard ya get up and . . ." He shrugged. "Well, I'll . . . mosey on back," he said. "G'night, Little Jack."

"Night," said Haskell.

Until the crunching sound of Melton's boots had faded, Little Jack remained motionless, staring at the cottonwoods on the opposite bank, listening to the soft gurgle of water over the stones. Thinking of how the sheriff had told him he'd better be on the watch because, sure as water ran, Kirk Baladine would be after him for gunning down his brother. He'd told the sheriff how it had been an accident, but the sheriff had only shaken his head and said, "Well, I'm afraid that don't make no difference now, son."

Little Jack sat down with a thud and stared at the moving

143

silver surface of the stream, his hands kneading harshly at each other.

"Was an *accident*," he murmured, wondering if he could tell Kirk Baladine what had happened and . . .

A shuddering sigh emptied from his lips. That was fool wishing.

His body went rigid as fury jolted through him. Why did it have to happen to *him*! He punched down savagely at the gritty soil and felt a flare of pain in the heel and little finger of his hand.

Up the slope a horse nickered and, suddenly, Little Jack scrambled around, jerked out his pistol, and thumbed back the hammer. A gasp tore from his lips as he remembered that the Colt was empty, and he pitched forward heavily onto the damp ground, lying there panting, wide eyes probing at the shadows.

It was just one of the corral horses spooking at a sound, a movement. Little Jack's hand slumped forward on his arm, breath shaking in him. His free hand struck at the ground slowly, feebly.

"Goin' in?" the men asked him Saturday evening.

"Naw," he said, "I'm done in." He managed a grin, but his stomach muscles were throbbing. He knew they all wanted to see him meet Kirk Baladine. He was their friend, but gunplay was a blind spot in that friendship.

"They'd send their own mother to a good shootin'," Melton had said, and it was almost true.

"Come on, Little Jack," one of them said, "I'll buy ya a drink."

"Naw," said Little Jack, "I'm . . . done in."

He couldn't think of anything else to say so he stared up at the bunk overhead, then closed his eyes and tried to

breathe evenly while the other men moved around in the
bunkhouse, getting ready to go into town. He wondered if
he should pretend to snore.

In the beginning, convincing himself that Kirk Baladine
wouldn't even hear about it, he'd enjoyed his notoriety. For
a man his age to kill an outlaw of Jed Baladine's rank was
a reputable act, and the ranch crew made him know it. He
was a celebrity and couldn't help being pleased by that. He
told the story of his fight with Baladine more than a dozen
times. But he always told it when Melton wasn't around.
"Man, nobody could've been more surprised than I was
when I got in the first shot! I just drawed and fired and down
he went!"

Then the sheriff had told him to watch out for Kirk
Baladine and now every enjoyment was coated with an icy
dread.

Little Jack lay in the empty bunkhouse, holding his pistol
tensely, every chamber loaded, the hammer cocked. For
hours he lay like that, snapping up to a sitting position every
time he heard a sound.

There was no point in practicing his draw anymore. He
was sure he'd never get any faster. The more he practiced
the more nervous he got until he started dropping the pistol,
his fingers made numb by fear.

Once, when a horse galloped into the ranch area, he blew
out the oil lamp and ran to the window in his stocking feet;
but it was only the owner of the ranch and, shivering, Little
Jack relit the lamp and sat down on his bunk again.

"Well, listen," he said suddenly in a loud, shaky voice, "it
was an accident. Was it *my* doin' he drawed on me? *Was* it?"
And he looked around quickly to see if anyone had heard.

When Melton came back at eleven and told him that Kirk
Baladine would be in town the next night, Little Jack sat

limply on his bunk, staring at his friend and not saying a single word.

Little Jack sat on his bunk rolling a cigarette. At the log table, two of the men were playing checkers while a third man watched. Across the dirt-floored room, Melton was cleaning his boots.

Little Jack ran his tongue along the paper and sealed in the tobacco. He pinched closed the ends, then raked a sulfer match along the wall, held it away from himself a moment, then lit the cigarette. Tossing aside the match, he lay back and blew up a cloud of smoke that hovered over him like a thinning wraith. He wiggled his toes slowly.

"Man, I'm—" he started, then broke off abruptly, knowing it would do no good. They were waiting for him to go. He yawned artificially and sighed, feeling a muscle twitch in his cheek. Each indrawn breath made his stomach muscles shake.

Well, I'm not going. He shuddered on the bunk, thinking, for a second, that he'd spoken the words aloud.

He drew in smoke and the tip of his cigarette glowed in the shadows. He saw his hand shaking and dropped it hastily to his side. He glanced at the men, feeling as if they were staring at him. When he saw that they weren't, he gritted his teeth and almost bit off the end of the cigarette. He turned his head back and stared at the butt of his Colt protruding from its worn leather holster. He wondered if it was clean enough. He started to get up to see, then fell back instantly and lay there tensely. He mustn't look at his gun. But what if it jams? he thought. He closed his eyes tight and wouldn't let himself think about it.

One of the men took out a watch and said, "Seven-thirty," to no one in particular it seemed. Little Jack felt his heart beat with a labored pulsing. He sat up slowly and ground the cigarette under his stocking heel.

"Well, I . . ." He swallowed quickly. "Guess I'll be goin'," he said, reaching for his boots.

One of the men at the checkerboard said, "Good move," to his opponent.

"Ya want me t'go with ya?" Melton asked.

Little Jack's face hardened. He saw one of the men look pointedly at Melton. Then he shrugged carelessly. "If ya want," he said, standing. "You—"

He caught himself, realizing he'd said the wrong thing. "No, never mind," he said quickly. "It's . . . my show."

The man looking at Melton nodded once and looked back at the checkerboard.

Little Jack could barely feel his fingers as he buckled on his gun belt. He bit into his lip and reached for his hat to hide the shaking of his body. Clapping the hat on, he sauntered for the door. He said, "See ya later," as he went out.

When the door was closed behind him, he stopped and pressed his eyes shut, hands closing into ivory-knuckled fists at his sides. He felt a drop of sweat run across his temple and down the side of his nose. He brushed it away and stepped off for the corral. They'd be listening for his bootfalls.

He was just swinging up onto his mount when he heard his name spoken. His hand dropped suddenly to his pistol butt and it was drawn before his body touched the saddle. Then he saw Melton walking toward him and shoved the pistol back into its holster.

"What d'ya want?" he asked tensely, when the big man had reached the horse's shifting side.

"I know this ain't my place, Little Jack," Melton said,

"but . . . well, why don't ya tell the sheriff what happened that night? Maybe he could—"

"No," Little Jack said, "it wouldn't do no good."

"But—"

"It's just got t'be this way," Little Jack interrupted. "That's all."

"But *you* didn't start it."

Little Jack shook his head. "That don't matter," he said.

He meant to ride off then, but he found himself talking instead.

"I been doin' a lot o' thinkin' on it," he said. "First off, I figured it was my own doin'. Like my old man used t'say; pride goes before fallin'—or somethin' like that. I figured it was my fault for not talkin' up—and it was, partly. But the way I see it now—it wouldn't have mattered none *what* I said. By the time the story got to Kirk Baladine, it'd be all wrung out o' shape anyway."

He drew in a chest-trembling breath. He knew his words sounded courageous and knew, at the same time, that he was only talking to avoid the inevitable. But he couldn't stop.

"And even if he heard it straight," he said, "it wouldn't matter none. It was still his brother I killed." He looked down at the big man. "No," he said, "I'm in a corner, Jack. And there ain't nothin' I can do about it."

They were silent a moment. Little Jack wanted desperately for Melton to keep him from going. But he knew it couldn't happen that way.

Abruptly, he laid the reins across the bay's cheek and it turned away. "S'long," he said.

"Ya want me t'go with ya?"

"*No.*" Little Jack's voice broke and, angry at himself, he kicked his boot heels against the horse's flanks and it broke into a gallop out of the ranch area. Even before he was out of sight of the bunkhouse light, he was sorry he hadn't said yes. Now the fear would pressure in him without a word to ease it.

As he rode toward town, Little Jack kept thinking about what he'd said to Melton, thinking how crazy it was that a man could sound so calm and brave and be so afraid. He blinked his strained eyes. He was tired, too. He hadn't slept for more than minutes the night before; writhing, turning restlessly, lying awake and listening to the other men snore peacefully. How could a man sleep when he knew he was going to be killed the next day?

And if he didn't go in? The thought occurred with sudden force. If he turned north and kept riding until he was out of the state, away from everything, what difference would it make? Why should he be forced to go into town and get himself shot? Wasn't honor a stupid thing when it demanded suicide?

Little Jack shook himself angrily, bleak eyes searching ahead for the town lights. Why think about it? He wasn't just Little Jack Haskell, alone and able to do what he pleased. Like every man, he lived in a circle of demands that had to be met.

The town seemed to jump out at him as if it had been hiding behind the night-shrouded bluff, waiting to pounce. One minute he was alone on the prairie, riding under a sprinkle of icy stars. The next, the town was moving past him on both sides, trapping him in its streets—and up ahead was the Latigo Saloon with one horse tied up in front of it.

Little Jack's body twitched and his heartbeat which had been a dull thump became a fist punching at his chest wall. I can't, he thought, I *can't*.

And, even thinking it, he drew up in front of the saloon, dismounted, and curled the reins around the hitching bar.

Inside the saloon, there was a heavy silence. Under the slatted doors, Little Jack could see the dark boots of a man standing at the bar and his hands tightened on the rough wood of the hitching bar. Then, after a second, they fell away to his sides and he ducked under the hitching bar, moving for the plank sidewalk. From the corners of his eyes, he saw men standing in the shadows of the buildings, waiting.

He stepped up on the walk, a cold sinking in his stomach. He hesitated a moment, swallowing the obstruction in his throat, then, abruptly, pushed open the batwing doors and stepped inside.

The man at the bar didn't turn. His dark hat was lying on the bar top, and Little Jack noticed how blond and curly his hair was. There was an almost empty bourbon bottle in front of him and both the man's hands were wrapped around a shot glass. Little Jack stood there tensely, waiting, while, behind the bar, a white-faced Kelly slid slowly out of sight.

The clock ticked hollowly, sounding just as it had the night he'd killed Jed Baladine. Little Jack inhaled quickly, hands curled and twitching at his sides. The man at the bar began pouring more bourbon into his glass.

"You Kirk Baladine?" Little Jack suddenly heard himself asking. He saw the man's hand start a little, and bourbon splashed on the bar. The man put down the bottle with a thump.

"Well, *are* ya?" asked Little Jack, his voice rising with angry fright.

The man at the bar turned slowly. Little Jack saw how taut his face was. He was going to say something; then he pressed his lips together and waited.

"You the one?" Kirk Baladine asked.

Little Jack felt as if his insides were turning to stone. His hands hung leaden and unusable at his sides. An icy shudder sprayed up along his spine. No, he thought, no, it was an accident. You don't understand, it was an accident!

"I'm the one," he said and felt his legs, unbidden, spread into a bracing V beneath him. "What are you going to do about it?" It was as if he stood apart, watching someone in his body performing this unbelievable play.

Kirk Baladine's hands drew up slowly from his sides, his fingers spread. . . .

"All right," he said in a bitter voice. "All *right*."

The pistol seemed to fly into his hand. Instinctively, Little Jack clawed at his Colt as Baladine fired. He heard the slug scorching by his left ear and, very calmly, as if he were target shooting, he squeezed the trigger and felt the pistol jolt twice in his grip.

Kirk Baladine thrashed back with a gagging cry and sat down heavily on the floor, the gun skidding from his fingers. He stared at Little Jack with eyes as rigid as marble. His right hand felt around with a palsied movement as if he were searching for a lost button. He touched the brass foot rail and closed his fingers over it. Then a sob of pain tore back the color-drained lips from his teeth.

"It's yours," he gasped hoarsely. "It's *yours*."

He sat there a moment longer with Little Jack staring at him. Then he slipped back with a deep sigh as if he were going to sleep for the night. Little Jack heard his head bump on the floor. He saw the outlaw's legs go rigid, then limp.

His boot heels thumped hollowly in the quiet of the saloon as he walked over to where Kirk Baladine lay. He stood there shuddering at the dead youth who was looking at him.

"Holy . . . jumpin' . . . Jehoshaphat!"

Gasping, Little Jack whirled to see Kelly standing in the back doorway gaping at Baladine. Kelly's wide eyes moved up to Little Jack's face.

"Ya done it," he said, his voice muted with awe. "Ya *done* it."

Then it was like the first time; Kelly rushing out into the street, shouting "Baladine's dead!" and the men coming in, slowly, then quickly, shaking Little Jack's hand, pounding him on the back, buying him drinks. The sheriff and the undertaker coming.

Except that it was different somehow. Little Jack kept thinking about Kirk Baladine's young face, of his tense voice, of the way he'd spilled whiskey from the bottle when he was spoken to, of the way he'd missed an easy shot even though he'd drawn first.

It wasn't until one of the men yelled, "Everyone's gonna be scared o' Little Jack now!" that Little Jack understood. *Kirk Baladine had been afraid of him.* He'd killed Kirk's older brother and that made him a frightening figure.

And now he'd killed Kirk Baladine, too. Little Jack stood numbly at the bar listening to the men talk about how he was going to be one of the most famous men in the territory. He'd downed two of the feared Baladines in one week. It didn't matter that the first killing was accidental, the second luck. Now he was famous; and now would come the challengers of his fame.

Suddenly, Little Jack knew exactly what the young outlaw had meant when he'd said, "It's *yours.*"

Like a dying monarch, Baladine had passed along the trouble of his kingdom.

Little Jack began to wait.

OF DEATH AND
THIRTY MINUTES

IT WAS TWO-THIRTY in the afternoon.

Old George was drawing two beers. He turned and pushed them across the counter to the cowhands. His clean stubby fingers slid the price from a pile of change. The two cowhands took long drinks. One of them rolled a cigarette and lit it. They both talked and chuckled in low voices.

The bartender's older son Len had just come in from the kitchen in back. His light brown hair was combed neatly. He had his arms twisted back tying the white apron strings behind him.

"Hello, Mickey," he said to his twelve-year-old brother, who was sitting at a back table polishing glasses.

Mickey looked up. "Hiya, Len."

"Mom says for you to be home in half an hour," Len said. "No later." He walked under the broad archway that led into the high-ceilinged barroom.

Jeanie was leaning against the piano. She was listening to the Maestro play a new song that had just come in from the East. She was going to sing it that night when the saloon got crowded.

The flowered dress she wore was an old one. It had a small tear in the right shoulder. She had a peach-colored silk shawl wrapped around her shoulders and upper arms. She was gazing at the long mirror behind the bar. As she listened to the music, her right hand tapped lazily on the piano top.

Len nodded to her, and her full red lips raised briefly in a smile. "Hello Maestro, Duke," Len said. The Maestro lowered his derby-topped head in a nod. Duke John was playing solitaire. Without raising his dark eyes, he grunted and reached out a lean, ringed hand for his cigar.

The bar was cool. The only sound was the tinny roll of the piano. Sunlight filtered through the faded colors of the window glass. A golden bar of it thrust underneath the swinging doors and ended a few feet into the saloon. The air smelled with food and liquor and polished wood.

Old George was sitting on his stool, reading the weekly paper. Jeanie hummed the song to herself. Duke John cheated without changing his expression. One of the cowboys yawned widely. In back, the boy polished glasses.

A horse came thudding down the street and pulled up at the hitching rail in front. No one paid any attention. Outside, boots sounded on the board sidewalk. The swinging doors were pushed open.

A lean young man of middle height came in.

His dark clothes and hat were whitish with powdery dust that clouded around him as he walked. He had a smooth-butt Colt .45 belted at his waist. It sagged down on one hip and the holster bottom was thronged to his leg. In the crook of his left arm he carried a double-barreled shotgun.

The two cowhands, Spence and Mack, glanced at the newcomer. Then they looked away. They didn't know him.

The young man stopped at the far end of the bar and leaned his shotgun against it. He twisted his shoulders forward wearily and then let them sag back. He plucked at the red bandanna around his neck and mopped the thick dusty sweat from his forehead, cheeks, and neck. He coughed once dryly and licked at his thin lips.

Old George had laid down his paper. He came shuffling up to the man.

"Yes, sir," he said. Automatically, he wiped the spotless bar surface with a damp rag.

"Whiskey," said the man. His voice was thin and hoarse. He pushed back the brim of his hat, and George saw a ragged scar over his right eye. The man had a two-days' growth of wiry, blond whiskers.

"Comin' up," said Old George. He moved back to the bottle shelves and picked one out. He brought it back with a shot glass and poured efficiently. The man watched the pouring whiskey with pale blue eyes. His chest rose and fell heavily.

"How about something to eat?" Old George asked the stranger.

The man took the shot glass in his claw-like right hand and threw down the whiskey in a gulp. His grimy face contorted. A cough puffed out his cheeks. Old George noticed a tic in his right cheek. "Water," the man gasped.

Old George moved down the counter and poured a glass. The man stood leaning heavily against the bar, breathing through a slightly open mouth. He stared at the dark glossy wood of the bar top.

He looked up suddenly. "Let's go!" he snapped, his voice strident. Spence and Mack glanced at him, and Jeanie gazed over sleepily. "Oh, keep playing," she said to the curious Maestro.

The glass of water was put down, and the man grabbed it up and gulped it down. Old George turned away.

"Whiskey," said the man.

He looked around the room as the drink was poured. He looked at everybody with expressionless eyes. His tongue moved slowly over his upper lip. Jeanie looked quickly back at the piano. The man stared at her. His hand on the counter opened and closed in uneven rhythm. His right boot tapped restlessly on the brass rail.

Old George moved away with the bottle. The man wrapped his right hand around the glass. With his left, he touched the barrel of his shotgun. His eyes never stopped moving around.

Len was arranging the sandwich tray near the back of the bar. Whenever the stranger's eyes were facing in a different direction, Len stared at his face. When he saw the scar, a look of concern crossed his face.

Old George put back the bottle and came up to Len.

"Son, run down the cellar and . . ." His voice broke off as he saw Len still looking at the man. "What's the matter?" he asked.

Len whispered. "Pa, do you know who that guy is?"

"No. Who?"

Len wiped his hands on his apron. "Don't you recognize his face? That scar over his eye?"

Old George looked impatient. "All right. *Who* is it?"

Len shuddered. "Not so loud, Pa," he cautioned and threw a glance over at the restless man standing at the end of the bar.

"It's Jake Warner," he whispered.

The old man's face tightened. He looked over his shoulder in alarm. "Don't look," Len warned. Old George's head moved back. His hands reached out and he rubbed the bar surface with his cloth.

Then he turned and pretended to check the labels on the

bottles. He tried not to look at the man who had now taken off his hat and dropped it on the counter. The man's dirty blond hair was plastered by sweat to his scalp and forehead.

"Are you sure, Len?" George whispered. "Dead sure?"

Len opened the cash box and pretended to count the money inside. "I tell you it's him," he insisted. "I pass the sheriff's office every day and the poster of Warner is right outside. I swear that's him at the end of the bar."

Old George put down a bottle. "We got to do somethin'," he said.

"We have to call the sheriff," Len said.

Old George clenched his fingers on the back shelf. He noticed in the mirror how pale he was. "I don't want no shootin' in here," he muttered. "*Can't* have it. Not with Miss Foster and the boy here."

Len bit his lip and shut the cash box. "Pa, we can't keep *talkin'* like this," he said. "He'll get suspicious. I'll go get the sheriff." He started to move away, but Old George grabbed his arm. "Pa, don't!" Len's face grew taut.

"*We can't have any shootin' in here.*"

Len swallowed. "I'll tell the sheriff to wait then," he murmured hurriedly. His eyes shifted down to the pistol that lay on the shelf under the bar. "Pa, do you think we could . . ."

"Don't be a fool!" his father warned softly. He glanced into the mirror and a chill ran down his back as he saw the young man watching him. The man's eyes were drained and colorless. They looked like the eyes of a dead man.

"Listen, you be sure to tell the sheriff he's got to wait," he said to Len. "He's *got* to wait till Warner leaves here."

"All right, I will, I will." Len began to undo his apron with shaking fingers. The bow knotted on him, and he drew in a hissing breath. Mack glanced over curiously.

"Never mind the apron," whispered his father, "just go on."

"How can I when . . . Pa, he's *looking* at us."

Old George took a deep breath and braced himself.

"That's right," he said in a normal voice, "take the tray into the kitchen." The rest he whispered "*And take the boy out with you!*"

"Yes, but . . ."

"Hey, *you!* Bartender!"

Old George stiffened. There seemed something deadly and unbalanced in the man's voice.

"Go on," George muttered as he turned to grab the bottle. He moved down the length of the bar, listening for the sound of Len's footsteps.

There was nothing. He stopped in front of the man and poured the drink, steeling his arm muscles to keep from spilling the whiskey. He felt the man's eyes on him. "Did I say another whiskey?" the man asked. George looked up nervously.

"What? Oh," he said, "I thought you . . . *wanted* another one." He felt his heart thudding heavily. Close up, the man looked deranged.

Mack called out. "Two more beers, George!"

Old George turned abruptly and moved away from the man. His harried eyes swept over to the back room. He saw Len there, talking to Mickey.

"Naw, I gotta finish these," Mickey argued loudly.

Old George thumped down the bottle. He grabbed the two steins and muttered to himself as he turned away. "Get *out* of here." He slapped over the spigot.

"Pa *said!*" Mickey protested angrily.

Old George jumped as the beer washed over the stein

edge and soaked his hand. Quickly, he stuck the other stein under the tap.

"What are you dreamin' about, George?" Mack laughed as the beer splattered on the sawdust-covered floor. Old George gritted his teeth together. The piano playing went on and on, its frail clatter filling the air. Mickey still argued.

George turned around, then slid the beers across the counter. Without control he looked at the back room again. Mickey was just getting up, a disgusted look on his face. He and Len were starting for the kitchen. George took a deep shivering breath.

"Hey! *You!*" The man's thin voice rang out over the piano.

The Maestro's hands lifted from the yellowed keys and the barroom was suddenly quiet. Old George saw his two sons hesitate, then stop, inches from the kitchen door. Mickey turned around. "Huh?" he said.

"You with the sandwiches," the man said. His face was almost blank. The tic pulsated in his right cheek and made him look as though he were winking.

"Get out here," he said. Duke John finally put down the deck and raised his eyes. Everybody was looking toward the far end of the bar. The man kept his eyes fixed on Len.

Len was moving into the big room slowly, holding the tray tightly with blood-drained hands. Mickey followed, asking, "What is it, Len? What does he want?"

"Get away from me," Len muttered out of the side of his mouth.

"Put down the tray," said the man, and Len slid the tray onto the bar.

Mickey stood in the archway staring at the man. "Pa?" he said, glancing toward his father, but Old George shook his head and hurriedly gestured for Mickey to be quiet.

"Come here," said the man. George kept his eyes on him and began to inch his way toward the shelf that held the pistol.

"What's up?" he heard the Maestro whisper.

Jeanie said, "How should *I* know?"

Len took a few hesitant steps toward the poker-faced man. He coughed once, nervously. "Yeah?" he said.

The man's foot slid off the rail and thumped on the floor. Both his hands on the counter opened and closed slowly. They looked like dusty brown spiders. Mack and Spence put down their beers and kept looking curiously at the man.

"Where do you think you're goin'?" asked the man. His voice was soft and it bubbled liquidly in his throat as if he hadn't swallowed all his drink.

Len cleared his throat. "I was going to the kitchen," he said.

"What were you talkin' about before?" The young man's voice still didn't rise, but it sounded as though it was going to rise. His fingers tapped loudly on the bar.

"We wasn't talkin' about anything," Len said.

The man was quiet. His eyes bored into Len's. Len stirred restlessly. "But people always talk about somethin'," the man said. "Nobody talks about nothin'." His shoulders twisted impatiently. "*What were you talkin' about?*" Now his voice was louder.

"We wasn't talkin' about anything," Len said.

"What were you talkin' about?" The man spoke slower. He seemed to be forcing his voice down because his chest moved faster and the tic in his cheek twitched more.

Old George spoke out. "We was talkin' about . . ." He stopped suddenly as the man's icy eyes fixed on him.

"What?" said the man. "What were you talkin' about?"

"*Nothin'*, I tell you," Len said loudly.

The man's right hand dropped off the counter. Len shuddered. He couldn't see the man's hand.

"What were you talkin' about?" asked the man.

Len tried to smile. "Look, mister," he said, "I don't see why . . ."

His mouth fell open in shock. The man had the .45 pointed at his chest.

"What are you doing?" he asked feebly.

The man picked up his hat and set it on his head. His voice was almost inaudible.

"I can't trust *nobody* anymore," he said, his eyes glittering. "It don't matter where I go. I just can't trust nobody." He cocked the hammer of his pistol.

"No, Warner!" Len threw up his hands and backed away.

The man's lips raised slowly and a thin chuckle hung in his throat. "You know me," he said. The chuckle rose. "Well, that's too bad. I don't like people who know me." He bent over slightly, picked up his shotgun, and began to back toward the door.

"Where do you want it, buddy," he asked as he edged back, "in the belly or in the face?"

A sob broke in Len's throat. "No," he muttered, throwing a pleading glance toward his father.

Old George grabbed the pistol from the shelf and fired.

Jake Warner lurched to his left and went down on one knee as the bullet tore through his leg. Falling, he threw up his right hand and explosions filled the room as the big gun jolted twice in his hand. Old George flung up his arms with a cry. The pistol flew from his hand and crashed against the mirror. A jagged chunk was knocked out and clattered down onto the shelf. Jeanie screamed, and everybody was suddenly standing up, staring at George.

He had both his hands pressed to his chest. Blood spurted

163

out between the fingers and splashed down over his white apron. "Len," he choked and staggered forward two steps. Then he disappeared behind the bar, his outstretched left arm sweeping Mack's stein off the counter. The report of the shattering glass broke the silence.

"Pa!" Thoughtless, Len turned and broke into a frantic run for the other end of the bar to reach his father.

Warner's gun roared again, and Jeanie threw one hand across her mouth in horror.

Len's head jerked wildly, and his body seemed to snap back around the point in his back where the bullet had crashed in. His right leg kicked up in the air as he flopped on his stomach with a gurgling cry. A few feet away, Mickey stood in numb shock, staring down at his brother.

Len dragged one clenched hand over the floor, a screeching whine of agony filling his throat. Spence took a step toward him.

"Don't move!" howled Warner.

Spence stopped and stared at Len as he lay gagging on the floor. He watched Len's body shudder and go limp. Then his head turned slowly until he faced the outlaw.

Warner was dragging himself across the floor, leaving the shotgun behind. His eyes seemed all whites. He kept his pistol wavering before him as he pulled himself up painfully by the edge of the bar. His yellow-toothed mouth hung open, and he sucked in whistling breaths.

"Anybody else?" he gasped hoarsely, grimacing. His shoulders twitched violently. "Anybody else?" he yelled at them. Then his head jerked back as he gasped and his hat fluttered down to the floor.

He dropped his gaze immediately and looked around. Suddenly he hopped over on one leg and fired another bullet into Old George's motionless body. "Bastard!" he yelled at the body. "Stupid bastard!"

He leveled his gun on the rest of them. Leaning forward, shoulders hunched, he stared at them. "Come *on*," he said brokenly. "Somebody make a move. Let's go, let's *go*!"

They were all still. Spence and Mack kept their hands hanging stiffly at their sides. Nobody moved.

"Let's *go*!" Warner threw back the hammer of his pistol with a convulsive movement.

Then they all heard shouting in the street. There were running boots on the wooden sidewalk. Jake Warner let go of the bar and lurched backward toward the doors.

"Gotta get out of here," he muttered to himself, eyes flashing over his shoulder.

Suddenly his left leg buckled and a cry of pain tore through his lips. He broke the fall with his left hand closed over the stock of his shotgun.

"Get your hands up!" he yelled, and everyone put their hands in the air. Warner pushed to his feet using the shotgun as a cane. He hobbled back to the doors and glanced over them. Throwing back one glance, he pushed out into the street.

Spence moved to Len's body and knelt beside it. His hand felt for the heartbeat. Mack broke into a run for the door.

Shots exploded outside. Warner suddenly came bursting back into the saloon, his face contorted with rage. Mack skidded to a halt and threw up his hands.

"Scum!" Warner yelled. He shoved open one door with his pistol barrel and fired two quick shots. Men outside fired back and two slugs splintered the doorjamb over Warner's head. Turning, he staggered away from the door, the stock of his shotgun thumping on the floor.

"Get back!" he yelled at them, his voice rising hysterically. He threw up his pistol at Mack and pulled the trigger. The gun clicked.

Warner's eyes dilated. Before Mack could move for his gun, Warner had thrown up the shotgun to fire. But his left leg buckled again and the roaring blast only tore up the floor in front of Mack's feet.

Mack threw up his hands and jumped back, his face twitching. "No, don't, don't," he begged.

Warner struggled up and, lurching over to the bar, fell against it heavily. He laid the shotgun across the counter. Then, with his eyes always on them, he put the pistol on the bar and feverishly pulled bullets from his belt. As he loaded, wheezing breaths puffed through his nostrils.

In a moment, he had snatched up the pistol again. His pale eyes flicked toward the back of the bar and held on Mickey. "Get *in* here!" he said and raised his gun.

"Mickey, come here," Jeanie said. Mickey edged across the floor, his dazed eyes still on his dead brother's body. Jeanie pulled him against her.

Warner glanced toward the door as two more bullets came digging into the saloon walls.

Duke John half stood. "*Idiots*. Don't they know there's a woman and boy in here?"

One of the doors flew open, and a rifle shoved through. Warner fired twice, and the legs under the door staggered and moved out of sight. Someone across the street shouted out, "Get away from there, you fool!"

Warner leaned against the bar again. Without looking, he felt for the glass. It was empty. He slid in behind the bar and limped back to the bottle shelves. There, he grabbed a bottle and went back to his place, teeth gritted in pain. He poured a drink and threw it down. Then he looked at all of them through half-closed eyes.

"Sit down," he slurred. "All of you, sit down. By that window. You!" He waved his pistol at Duke John. "Put more chairs there."

Duke John kept his black eyes on Warner as he dragged chairs across the floor. Warner kept glancing toward the door, his weight still resting on the bar.

Jeanie sat down and held her arm tightly around Mickey's waist. Her large eyes were fastened on Warner's sweating, pain-etched face. Duke John sat down. The Maestro cautiously pulled his piano stool to the table. Spence and Mack started away from the bar.

"Both of you," Warner said, "drop your gun belts."

A man shouted from the street. "You in there!"

"It's the sheriff," the Maestro whispered.

"Don't any of you move," Warner ordered. He grabbed his shotgun and stumbled painfully to the door. "You make a move," he warned over his shoulder, "and I'll kill every last one of ya."

The sheriff yelled, "Whoever you are, come out with your hands up!"

Warner leaned against the wall by the door. His face paled as a burning fire ran up his leg. He looked back at Mack and Spence through pain-clouded eyes.

"Bring *him* here!" Warner pointed his pistol at Len's body.

They all stared at Warner. "*What?*" Spence said incredulously.

Warner fired into the floor. "I said *bring* him here!"

The two cowboys moved backward toward the body. Mack's face went white as his boot crushed down one of Len's outstretched fingers.

"Get him here," Warner said, gesturing with the pistol.

They bent over and dragged up the body, their faces

blank. They began to carry it toward Warner. Len's boot toes squeaked over the floor and great blood drops splattered on the floor behind his body. Jeanie turned Mickey's face away and pressed it against her cheek.

"Drop him," Warner said. They put Len's body down as gently as they could and it lay still in the thin glow of sunlight that came under the door.

"What are you gonna do?" Spence asked.

Warner cocked his pistol. "Get back," he said, and they edged away from him.

"Give yourself up!" the sheriff yelled outside.

Warner leaned the shotgun against the wall and bent over gasping to hook his fingers under Len's belt.

"Warner, you swine," Duke John said. Warner slipped to one knee. His gun jerked up and cannoned a slug through the window behind them. They all ducked.

"Sit down, I tell ya!" Warner shouted.

He forced himself up and dragged the body with him, teeth grinding together at the fiery pain in his leg. He held the body against the door and then, shoved. They saw Len's corpse go flopping onto the sidewalk. Warner hopped back and pressed himself against the wall as shots rang out in the street.

Then someone yelled, "Stop! That's Lennie Wade!"

Dead silence filled the street and bar. Warner leaned over and yelled, "Clear the street or I'll kill *everyone* in here!" He sucked in breath. "*Ten minutes!* I'm giving you ten minutes!"

There was a rumbling of voices. "Get him!" shouted one man.

"Hold it!" ordered the sheriff. There was a pause. Then the sheriff called, "Who *are* you?"

The outlaw smiled crookedly.

"Warner!" he yelled. "Jake Warner!"

In the street, everyone stopped talking at once. Warner chuckled to himself. He looked back at the people sitting at the table, his shoulders moving back with, almost, pride. "Warner," he muttered to himself. Then he turned back to the door, the amusement gone.

"Ten minutes!" he yelled.

He picked up his shotgun and limped back to the bar, glancing up at the big clock over the archway. "I give 'em too much time," he muttered. Then he shrugged and a twisted grin flitted over his face. For one moment he looked like a wicked, excited boy.

"He's insane," Jeanie murmured in a tault voice.

"He is," Duke John said as Warner looked over from the bar.

"Get off your guns," he said. He sounded more assured. "Drop 'em on the floor."

Mack and Spence stood up slowly. "*All* of you," Warner said.

The Maestro jumped up and held wide his suit coat. "I got no gun," he insisted. "See? Look for yourself. I got no gun."

Warner's gaze moved to Duke John.

Duke John spoke coldly. "I am unarmed," he said.

"You better be," Warner said, and the Maestro glanced nervously at Duke John. He saw the bulge in Duke John's coat where the small pistol lay under his armpit. Then he looked away quickly, his scrawny throat contracting.

The two gun belts thudded to the floor. "Kick 'em over," Warner said. Spence and Mack put their boot toes under the bunched leather and shoved. The holsters and belts skidded across the floor and Warner, reaching out with the shotgun barrel, fished them in. He made a pile at his feet.

Then he gasped again and slit his eyes. Gritting his teeth,

he pushed himself up and sat on the edge of the bar. Blood ran down his leg, over the dusty leather of his boot, and dripped off the brass rail. The Maestro stared at the dark drops rolling over the brass and dripping slowly to the floor.

It was deathly quiet in the barroom. They could hear each other's breathing. Their eyes were on Warner. They watched him wipe the back of one dirty hand across his brow. They watched him pick up the bottle and bolt down a mouthful of whiskey. They heard his right bootheel thump against the bar. Outside, the murmur of the crowd was a soft buzzing.

"They better get out of there," Warner said menacingly, as though the silence bothered him. His voice was tight and controlled. Duke John noticed how the pistol shook in his hand.

Warner inhaled heavily. Then, impulsively, he cocked the hammer of his pistol and pointed it at each one of them as if picking out one to shoot. His face twitched with struggling bravado as most of them pressed back instinctively into their chairs.

Duke John sat motionless, impassive. Warner held the pistol longest on him. His finger stroked the trigger. The pupils of his eyes seemed to disappear in the milky whiteness. Jeanie caught her breath.

Warner's eyes shifted to her.

"You," he said, "come here."

She pushed back. "Why?" she asked.

The pistol moved slightly until it was leveled at Mickey. "Come here or I'll blow off his head," Warner said. His voice cracked in the middle of the sentence. For a split second he sounded like a fierce boy who was pretending to be a man.

Duke John began to stroke the table with his long fingers.

"Get over here!" Warner yelled.

Jeanie stood up quickly. Duke John moved forward in his chair, but she dropped a restraining hand on his shoulder. "No, don't," she begged, "I don't want anyone else killed. Not because of me. Here, take Mickey." Duke John slowly put his right arm around the trembling boy.

Jeanie held her arms crossed over her chest as she moved across the floor toward Warner.

"Let's go," said Warner.

She stood before him and smelled the dust and sweat on his clothes. A cloud of his stale breath reached her nostrils and made her mouth twitch. She stood motionless, trying to return his unblinking gaze.

Then, almost casually, Warner raised his pistol and shoved it hard against her right breast. She gasped and froze in her tracks.

"Scared you, didn't I?" he said.

She shrank back a little, and he pushed the gun against her again and fingered the trigger. Her hands fell trembling to her sides. "No," she said feebly, almost without sound.

Warner pulled back the pistol and snickered. "Scared you," he said. He looked over at Duke John.

Then he turned back to Jeanie. "Put that shawl on my leg," he told her.

Shivering, she took the shawl off her shoulders. Warner poked at her dress with the gun barrel. "Got a rip," he said. She winced as the warm metal touched her skin, and the shawl fluttered down, draping itself over Warner's boot.

"On my leg!" he shouted in her face.

Hurriedly, she bent over and pulled the shawl off the boot with shaking fingers. She started to wrap it around the oozing wound just over Warner's calf. She felt his eyes running over her body, down the deep cut of her bodice. It made her shudder.

171

"How would you like to get killed?" Warner asked her and ran the gun barrel edge over the back of her neck. She gasped and her hands twitched on his leg. "Tie it right," he said quietly, "or else I'll blow out your brains."

As she tied, her body shuddered with sobs. Duke John watched in stony silence, his stomach muscles drawn in taut. They all watched in silence. "Not so tight," Warner said.

"Warner!"

His leg twitched, and he turned his head toward the door. Jeanie straightened up and took a step backward.

"Give yourself up, Warner!" yelled the sheriff.

"Oh, *no*," the Maestro said.

Warner's cheek began to pulse again. "Why, you dirty . . ." he started. His thin lips clamped together. Sliding off the bar suddenly, he shot out his left hand and plunged it into Jeanie's light-reddish hair. She cried out in pain as his hand tightened and he jerked her toward him.

Duke John's hand twitched on the table, but Jeanie was between him and Warner. He pushed Mickey from him gently. "Take the boy," he told the Maestro quietly.

"What are you going to do?" whispered the Maestro.

"*Take* him."

He watched tensely as Warner half-dragged Jeanie across the barroom floor. Warner's face was mad with pain and frenzy. Duke John's hands moved on the table.

Warner shoved Jeanie against the door and twisted the hair on her scalp until her lips wrenched open in an agonized cry.

"Tell the sheriff you're all gonna get killed if he don't do like I say," Warner's voice grated. "He's got two minutes. *Tell* him!"

Breath caught in her throat. She coughed. "Go on!"

Warner raged, poking her savagely in the back with the gun.

She cried out. "Sheriff!" Outside, the murmuring voices stopped abruptly. Duke John took his right hand from the table and rested it in his lap.

"Is that you, Jean Foster?" the sheriff asked.

"Yes, yes. Please. You've got to let him go."

"But . . ."

"Please! He'll kill us all!" she cried. "He said he would. He's already killed Lennie and Mr. Wade!"

Warner's fingers flexed in her hair and the edges of his mouth twitched up for a second.

"Who's in there with you, Miss Foster?" asked the sheriff.

"There's . . . s-six of us," she called. "Mickey Wade is here. He's just a . . ." She gasped as her head was jerked back.

"You hear that?" shouted Warner. "You got two minutes!"

There was a pause. "All right, Warner," said the sheriff. "But I warn you not to harm anyone else."

"*Two* minutes!"

Warner turned and flung her away.

As she landed on one knee, Duke John pushed up and jerked the pistol from under his coat and fired once. Warner grunted and spun halfway to the left. As he fell back against the wall, his big gun exploded twice and Duke John's frail body jackknifed over without a sound. His gun clattered down and he thudded to his knees, fell forward, and rolled over once on his back. Jeanie caught her breath and slumped forward in a faint.

Mickey tried to pull away from the Maestro. "No, Mickey," the Maestro entreated, "don't do nothin'."

Jake Warner pushed away from the wall and staggered across the floor, his left arm hanging limp. Blood pumped from the hole in his shoulder and ran down his arm to drip from his curled fingers. He almost fell as he came toward them.

"*Trick* me, huh?" He almost sobbed. "Well, I'm gonna kill all of ya. You think you're gonna get out of here alive? I'll kill you and you and . . ." He shook blood drops from his hand furiously.

Then his head snapped around and he made a drunken rush for the pistols on the floor. As he skidded down on one knee, his pistol dropped from his hand and a blank dazed look crossed his face. He shook his head dizzily and dug his teeth into his lower lip, a violin-like whine hanging in his throat.

Suddenly he grabbed up Spence's pistol and burned his gaze at Duke John's body. His teeth showed between his white lips, rows of yellow-stained enamel drawn tight.

"I am unarmed!" he croaked wildly. He fired into Duke John's body, emptied the gun into him, screaming at the jolting body.

The pistol clicked and he hurled it away. As it skidded into the back room, he snatched up his own pistol and pulled himself up. The room still echoed with the ringing shots. The Maestro sat gaping unbelievingly at the bullet-torn body. "Oh my God," he muttered to himself, "how can so many people die at once? I never seen so many people die at once. How can it happen?" His right arm slipped from Mickey's shoulder, but Mack noticed and grabbed the boy's arm to hold him still.

"Warner!" The call came from the street.

The wounded outlaw stumbled back to the door, his boot stamping over the hem of Jeanie's dress. "You better," he muttered. "You just better." He sucked in a sobbing breath and leaned against the wall. His left hand clenched.

"That's one more!" he shouted out. His throat contracted. "You got a minute!" He loaded his pistol again quickly.

He turned and looked at them. "Can't . . . kill . . . all of ya," he gasped. He forced a smile on his lips. "Gotta save ya." Abruptly he stared at the floor and looked as if he was afraid he might start to cry. His hands fixed themselves like molded claws.

Spence got up cautiously and started to edge toward Jeanie, who still lay on the floor. "Let me pick up . . ." he started to say.

"Get back!" yelled Warner. He fired without aiming, and the bullet tore a shallow slash through Spence's left shoulder. The cowboy clapped his right hand over the wound.

"I was just . . ."

Warner wasn't listening. He was rolling his head back and forth against the cool wall. "Let's *go*, let's *go*," he was sobbing hoarsely, fighting back tears.

He caught himself and looked at them. He drew in a deep breath and exhaled shakily through his distended mouth. He looked down at his blood-caked left hand.

"Half a minute!" he yelled, his voice cracking.

Spence helped Jeanie down into the chair. Her lips stood out like crimson gashes on her white face as she regained consciousness. "Thank you," she murmured.

Warner paid no attention. He talked to himself as he limped back to the bar. His voice trembled. "One more drink and I'm leavin'," he said. "One more drink."

He reached the bar and winced as he fell against his left arm. Suddenly he shoved the pistol into his holster and moved forward, glaring at all of them.

"See? The gun's in my holster! Somebody make a move." He shook his head dizzily, his throat contracting. He coughed. "Go on!" he croaked. "Go on, I tell ya!" He turned back toward the bar, eyes suddenly watering. His stumbling was like that of an old man, pathetic in pride. "I'm Jake Warner," he muttered brokenly. He shook uncontrollably.

Reaching out his shaking hand, he poured whiskey into the glass. It washed over the top and formed a murky puddle around the glass. Warner flung the bottle aside dramatically. It bounced on its thick bottom and slid across the floor, spouting whiskey.

A violent fit of coughing seized Warner as the liquor burned down his throat. He dropped the glass and pressed his back against the bar edge. He tried to keep his eyes open, but they filled with tears. He jerked out his pistol and it wavered in his grip as his thin chest vibrated with coughing.

They all sat motionless, watching him.

Finally the coughing eased and Warner raised his tear-filled eyes to them. He forced himself to raise his blood-coated left hand and brush the tears away. His breathing was labored and noisy.

"I don't like people who know me," he rambled hoarsely. He took a deep breath. "I'm gonna kill all of ya. Ya think I care about killin'? You think I'm scared to . . ." The sentence petered out. He extended the pistol and leveled it on Spence.

"Warner!"

The outlaw's head snapped toward the door. His face was blank.

"The street is clear!" called the sheriff.

Warner's face suddenly relaxed. A sob pushed uncontrolled from his lips. Then, realizing it, he willed the look of cold detachment back to his face. He looked at Mack.

"Come here, you," he said.

"What?" Mack's arm tightened on the boy's shoulders.

"Come here!" Warner rasped, saliva flecking his lips. He

fired once into the floor at Mack's feet, and Mickey cried out as the splinters drove into his legs.

Mack stood up quickly and pushed the boy over to Jeanie. He started across the floor.

"What do you want?" he asked.

Warner struggled to sound important. He carefully controlled his voice. "You think I'm goin' out alone?" he said. "I know sheriffs."

He shoved the pistol into Mack's stomach and pushed him toward the door. "You're goin' out first," he said. Then he stopped. "Give me my hat." Mack picked it up and handed it to Warner, who went white as he put it on with his left hand. The outlaw forced strength into himself and grabbed the shotgun. He limped behind Mack toward the door.

"Why do you—" Mack started and broke off with a shudder as Warner poked him with the pistol.

At the door, Mack hesitated.

"Get out," Warner said.

"But what if—"

"Get out before I blow off your head!"

Mack swallowed. Then, as Warner punched him with the pistol end, he pushed out through the doors, throwing up his hands and calling out, "Don't shoot me!"

Warner pressed himself to the doorjamb and watched, his back turned to the rest of them.

"Anyone out there?" he asked hurriedly.

"No," came Mack's answer, "they're all down the street."

"Untie my horse," Warner said. "Don't try anything. I can see you good."

They all heard Mack's hesitant steps on the sidewalk. Then the whinny of a horse. Warner drew in a rasping breath. "Bring him in here!" he called.

"*What?*"

"You heard me!"

There was an uneven clatter of hooves on the plankwalk.

"He won't come!" cried Mack.

"*Pull* him!" Warner slid the pistol into his holster and turned completely away from the rest. He held one of the doors open. "*Come* on, boy, *come* on," he urged, his unaffected voice almost boyish with fright. "Come on, boy. In here!"

The clatter of hooves was louder. Spence stood up in one movement and took a hesitant step toward the holsters lying on the floor. Jeanie tightened. "What is he—" Mickey started to ask, but she put a hand over his mouth.

Warner wasn't looking back. "In here, boy!" he was entreating his horse. He sobbed. "Bring him in, I tell you!" Outside, Mack struggled with the twisting horse.

Spence took two more steps toward the holsters. He moved in a crouch.

Suddenly the batwing doors were flung open by the horse's chest. One of them went crashing into Warner's left side and, with a howl of pain, he reeled back and fell sprawling across a table.

Spence dove for Mack's pistol. Dropping to his knees, he jerked it from its holster and threw up the barrel. Warner's snap shot shattered the clock face in back.

Spence pulled the trigger.

His mouth fell open in horror as the hammer clicked on an empty chamber. He pulled again. There was no explosion.

Warner struggled to his feet, face red and contorted. He fired at Spence, and the bullet knocked Spence's right leg out from under him. Mack dragged at the horse as it backed out of the saloon.

Warner braced himself and tried to aim carefully.

A gun exploded once, again. Warner staggered under the impact and his mouth fell open. The gun slipped from his fingers and crashed onto the floor. He took a drunken step toward the door. "Gotta get out," he muttered weakly. "Here, boy." Blood flowed down his chest as he pushed out through the swinging doors and his boots staggered over the sidewalk.

Two more shots rang out, and they all heard him scream once. Then his body went splashing into the water trough in front of the next building.

Jeanie stood immobile, Duke John's pistol held level in her hand. The Maestro sat openmouthed and shaking in his chair. Mickey edged toward the back room. There, he turned and ran out through the kitchen. No one saw him leave.

Spence sat on the floor still holding the empty pistol and staring blankly toward the door.

Jeanie put the pistol on the table and sat down quietly.

Mack came running in. "They got him!" he said. He looked at Spence. "Are you all right?" he asked.

Spence looked up dizzily. "Ya might load your gun," he muttered.

"Huh?"

Spence shook his head. Jeanie put her arms on the table and slumped forward onto them, her back rising and falling with heavy breaths.

The Maestro reached up to take off his derby. It fell from his nerveless fingers and rolled in a half circle on the floor.

"My God," he said.

Outside, men shouted.

It was three o'clock in the afternoon.